White Nights
Białe noce

White Nights
Białe noce

stories by
Urszula Honek

translated by
Kate Webster

—— MTO PRESS
WIVENHOE 2023

Contents

White Nights
Białe noce

Permission to Land

A house like a chicken coop, so that if you leaned on it or kicked at it, all the planks would fall to the ground, and some would break in half, everything rotten. How it didn't collapse on their heads over the years, I don't know. Maybe they walked on tiptoe and didn't cry out when they fucked, or when they had bust-ups, otherwise I don't get it. Plus the house sits on the very edge of the hill, right next to the turn-off to Rożnowice. If you drove past in a lorry, you could high-five Pilot as he leaned out of the window. Everything inside must have been shaking when they were eating or sleeping, I wouldn't have coped with it for that long, but what can you do if you've got no choice? And there was just the one main room, plus a kitchen and the crapper outside, and twelve mouths to feed – well, eleven and a half, cos Pilot only counted as half. Did I use to go there? Not much, only once or twice when I was little, Pilot and Andrzej would come to ours, or more often we'd play in the field, in the scrubland or Grodzki woods. But there's one time I was there, I remember it, and I was maybe five years old. The entrance was more like a shed than a house, dirt beneath your feet, straw poking out from the walls and hanging from the ceiling, the plaster flaking, but that's not what I remember most. The first time, I was scared of the dark, cos you entered in broad daylight and in there it was night, no windows in the hallway, only in the kitchen opposite, but it seemed distant and bright, like it wasn't part of the house. I don't know if that was all real, but I reckon I was onto something. Now it seems to me that when my time comes – and I'm the only one left of the three of us – I'll walk down that hallway to my end.

Maybe if Pilot hadn't been so hung up on that pond and that girl, he'd still be here.

The sun goes down gradually here, it's not like you count to three and it's suddenly so dark you can't see your hand in front of your face. To begin with, the trees disappear into the gloom, then the roofs of the houses, the windows, the people, and finally the cows in the fields. The world turns red like it's caught fire. You fear it slightly, but then a deep blue starts to show through, trying to extinguish the flames, steadying the heart. Every summer here starts and ends like this, unless it's pouring with rain, then it's ashen, as if people had taken dust from the coal wagons and sprayed it into the air, that's how I've imagined it since I was a kid. When it's pouring, sometimes storks come out onto the waterlogged meadows and sink their skinny legs in so deep that they can't move, it's a funny sight. The foxes – I like them the best – are keener to stick their heads out of their burrows, and by day they start toing and froing like taxis in the city centre. The redness confuses the humans more than the animals, they look up at the sky more often than usual, then clench their fists and keep walking, but if you stopped them and asked: "Where'd you go?", they couldn't tell you. They'd just stand there, like they'd been roused from a deep sleep, their mouths open. On days like that, Pilot would go up the hill with a shovel and see where he could start digging. He'd stand still in the red landscape and crane his neck.

He started from the north.

"I'll get going on the pond from the edge of Firlit's field," he said suddenly outside the shop, with his frog-like cackle.

Nothing else, just that one sentence. His head was usually tilted backwards, but when he laughed it looked like he was about to fall over, cos his head went even further back, almost as far as his arse.

"Hey, Pilot, you're fit for the circus, you could do backwards somersaults," people would say, and I don't think he realised they were taking the piss out of him.

At one point, I even saw him practising fucking gymnastics! Not as a child, he was already getting on a bit. I dropped round cos he hadn't been at the shop for a few days, and he was usually there day in, day out, but his front door was closed. So I looked in the shed and there he was, touching his toes and doing star jumps. I was speechless. Had he been hiding away since he was a kid and dreaming of running off to join the circus? Of course, we all have dreams, but he's quite skinny, a bit of a runt, and not too agile. He could dig wells, I'm not gonna lie, he got work when he wasn't drinking, and there'd been no complaints there, but he wasn't cut out for acrobatics. When he jumped, his feet barely left the ground and he fell over seven times out of ten. I stood there and I couldn't stop watching him, one minute I wanted to laugh, the next I wanted to cry, it didn't make sense.

The first time that happened with him – that I was sad and happy all at once – was when we were little, maybe in the second year of school. Sometimes he went to school, but more often he didn't, he wouldn't show up for weeks, then he'd come back for a bit, he never learned to read well, could barely write his own name. Since Andrzej and I were his closest friends, the teachers asked us: "Where's Mariusz?", cos that was Pilot's name. But we just lowered our heads and shrugged to say we didn't know – and that was the truth. We thought his folks had put him to work and weren't letting him go to school, but it turned out that wasn't it. He left the house every day, slinging his bag over his shoulder, even saying "go with God" to his mother, cos that's what everyone here was taught to do, but he didn't make it to the school gates. Instead, he lay in the ditches for six or seven hours, or hid in the bushes, and when word got out, he came to school black and blue. I don't think his folks had ever beaten the shit out of him like that, though they did beat him regularly. And when someone asked why he'd been gone for so long and where those bruises and scabs had come from, he'd say that he'd gone to war, he was guarding the trenches, darting around the forests with the partisans. And that was the first time I got tears and laughter together. And now I wonder whether maybe he wasn't making it up, maybe he really had seen war, defended his homeland, and shot at the enemy for his mother and father? Who the hell knows. I'll be honest: I lived in Germany for a few years, and everyone knows they made lampshades from human skin, but still, people like Pilot are respected there now, welfare, nurses, clean hospitals, scented toilet paper, and the kind of sick pay where you don't need to do anything ever again. That's how it should be here too, not just all hype and no action. That kind of illness is even worse than when you've lost a leg, cos you can't see it, they're just plodding along, but they feel like they're flying above the earth. Pilot had always been like that, he'd suddenly stop talking and just stare into space. You could talk to him, but by that point he'd flown somewhere far away and he seemed to feel better there, cos for a long time he wouldn't want to come back. But when he said he was going to dig a pond, he laughed, and louder than usual, right from his core, like his insides were shaking. I'd only heard him laugh like that once before, twenty years earlier, when I let him ride my motorbike. At the time, his reaction surprised me, but now that I'm older and the lads are gone, I get it. So when he'd said about the pond, he fell silent, stared into the distance, then got up and left without a word.

He started digging on the most beautiful morning.

I'm not really sentimental, but he couldn't have picked a better day. You'd have to live here for a while, wake up here in the morning, to know. Anyone who has to travel to work is gone by six. It gets quiet, the cows are given water and led out, they're in the fields, the children still in their beds, little movements here and there, cos they're stirring, restless, knowing they have to get up for school soon. Chilly in short sleeves, but so nice, like climbing out of a cold river and hugging a naked woman's body; but the most beautiful thing is the light, I haven't seen a light like that anywhere in the world, and I've been a few places. It's like you're looking through steam hanging in the air, everything's a bit blurry, but getting brighter by the second, and you can hear bees and flies, and grasshoppers ticking in the grass. It might sound funny, but that's how it is. I was laden down, cos someone wanted a pig slaughtered. I headed towards the upper road, where Pilot and Andrzej and I used to go sledging, and after a while I turned right. The journey was going well, I slowed my step to take a look at the world around me, cos I liked what I saw, I even thought that I could stay forever, I'd bring Anka, she didn't need to work, we'd make a living from what we had. I've got the job I've got, no plans to quit, you can't lose heart. I don't think I've ever again felt what I felt then, but there's no point talking about it, after that it all fell apart. Pilot was already standing in the pit he'd dug, three feet square, smiling from ear to ear; at first he stood out against the light, silence and warmth that was slowly thickening in the air, but then I realised it was the opposite – he actually fitted in like never before.

"Hey, Pilot, you digging a fucking grave or what?" I shouted to him, cos he was standing lower down, I was up above him on the hill. And he'd chosen a good place, I thought. Wetland, maybe it would work.

"There'll be carp here in two months!" he shouted back to me, picking up the shovel and waving it like a flag, he kept laughing, the last time he was that happy was on the motorbike, like I said, he'd bared his toothless gums then as well.

He kept his word – he dug flat out for a month and a half, he stopped coming to the shop, it was a sign he'd either gone on a bender or he was getting down to business. He didn't want any help with the digging from me and Andrzej.

"I have to do it myself, so it's mine most of all," he explained, and halfway through June he invited us to the pond. "Come tomorrow, we'll release the carp, everything's ready," he said, and after that he didn't pipe up again, though we sat drinking together for a good three hours.

But it turned out that everything wasn't ready, cos in the

morning he arranged for Jabłonowski to drive him to Folusz for the fish, and that's quite a way, some fifteen miles from us. I don't know how he got that fucker to do it, must have paid him good money, but Jabłonowski arrived as promised, in his chunky blue Nysa police van so he wouldn't have to pay for petrol, and he probably thought he'd be transporting big barrels of carp, but Pilot came out holding two buckets filled with water.

This was a big day for Pilot. Of course, he'd seen people build houses, get married, have children, and he wanted to make an impression with his pond. And the pond was a decent size, I'm not gonna lie. Eighty feet square, and eight feet deep, from what I could tell. When I arrived in the late afternoon, Pilot was still on his own. He stood staring at the murky water, holding the buckets of fish.

"When Andrzej and the others get here, we'll release them," he said, excited.

"Who else is coming?" I asked.

"Some girls," he said more quietly.

"What girls? Are they pretty?"

"Dunno, Andrzej invited them. One is, for sure…"

Of course it was Andrzej who invited them, I thought, cos if it was you, not even a lame dog would've come, but I did feel ashamed for thinking that. I walked over to Pilot, who was squatting now by the pond, and I patted him on the back, then I plucked up the courage to hug him, for the first and last time in my life. Had anyone ever hugged him with real feeling? Maybe when he was born? Though not necessarily. He was let out of the house like a cat, and was supposed to stay out.

"Your pond is the best around, from Folusz to here, and no one's ever dug one like this on their own," I told him.

"Cut the crap," he replied, confused but clearly pleased. "Seriously, it's true."

Andrzej came staggering down the hill, followed by his sister Henia, who always clung to him like a leech, and three other girls, one from the village and two from Ołpiny. They were my best friends, Pilot and Andrzej, and I didn't respect one more than the other. But sometimes I envied Andrzej, cos whenever we went out, the girls would swarm around him. But line the three of us up next to each other, and if I were a girl, there'd be no contest. Andrzej, tall, slim, his hair thick and dark, his hands strong and somehow smooth, and strangely deep blue eyes, almost like my Anka's – you look into them and you disappear. I don't know how he kept his hands like that, I guess he did everything in gloves, well, you can cut down a tree with gloves on, but you gotta hold pigs with your bare hands, then you separate everything with your fingers, membranes, fat, tendons, no other way to do it. If I were him, I'd take advantage of it, a different bird at every party, but I guess he didn't want to or he'd lost heart, and as I said, you need a heart for everything: working and fucking. Everyone knows he was in love with the Konieczny girl, but she was much younger, fifteen I think, so not ideal. People talked a lot, old Konieczny got pissed off, and then when their youngest daughter went missing, but not the one he liked, she was even younger, everyone was suspicious of Andrzej, though the police couldn't prove anything. I was gone by then, I'd moved abroad, but those kinds of things always get back to you, even if you're in outer space. I don't know if it's okay to talk this way about the deceased, but even before that, Andrzej would lose the will to live every now and then. He'd hang himself or take pills, he'd been saved a few times, but the last time, when I was already living in Germany, he wasn't. And they found that little girl twenty miles away, someone else had killed her. I've thought about it so many times, usually when I couldn't get to sleep: what was going through his head as he went out into the dark night, or the early morning, as he searched for the thickest branch, I don't know, I really don't. Was he crying or were his eyes dry? Or maybe there was nothing left inside, like a corpse? That seems the most likely to me, cos sometimes when you looked at him, you'd come over all cold, like if you went out in February in just your flip-flops.

But back then, it was still the three of us sitting by the pond.

"Pilot, let's get a move on with the carp," I said, cos I'd noticed they were moving less and less in the buckets.

He pulled one of them out, I think he only had six, two were barely alive, and he wanted me and Andrzej to release one each as well. He was excited by it, it was obvious, his hands were shaking and he started to stutter a bit. Other than that, I don't remember much about that night, but two weeks later, on a Saturday, Pilot turned up all smartly dressed, freshly shaved, his hair combed, and with almost clean nails.

"Let's go to the dance in Ołpiny, I'm meeting someone there," he said in a confident voice.

"Fuck's sake, Pilot, you've gotta give us some warning for stuff like that! Who are you meeting there, anyway?" I asked.

"What do you mean who, you know perfectly well who, so you can stop with the questions," he replied, offended. "Who was there at the pond? Or have you fucking forgotten already?"

"Ah, them," I said.

"One of them," he said more quietly. "Her with the blonde, curly hair."

"It was dark, I didn't see who had what hair, and I don't give a shit. We'll go. You're lucky I've got nothing better to do."

There's not much reason to go to Ołpiny, it's quite flat, and personally, I like a little hill here and there, and I especially like forests surrounded by huge meadows, so that when you emerge from the undergrowth, you can suddenly see a lot of light, colours, haystacks, a rake leaning against them, and then you're not afraid of the world anymore, cos you know that someone's there, even if you can't see them. I never told anyone about it, but later, when I'd got Pilot and Andrzej jobs and I moved in with Anka, I'd often start up my little Maluch and go for a drive by myself, to places where there's nothing, no houses, only a few bricks sticking out here and there, or withered apple trees, which once upon a time must have had firm, juicy apples, and someone's hand would place them in a basket. If you've never been somewhere like that, you have to see it, I couldn't stay there, probably only Andrzej could, but anyone who's thought that much about croaking can't be far off salvation. Maybe he was already walking arm in arm with the dead in that strange silence that I was starting to fear, who knows?

There was no dance in Ołpiny – or rather, there was, but a week before, Pilot had fucked up the dates. We were standing in the empty square near the fire station, where dozens of pairs of legs had been pounding out a rhythm the previous week. It was windy, a piece of rag was blowing back and forth across the square, Pilot was circling like he wanted to confront the invisible dancers, touch their shoulders and see if that blonde beauty of his might eventually look at him. He returned with his head lowered, he didn't even want to smoke, he got out of the car in front of his house without a word. I looked in the rear-view mirror for a long time: he was standing there, his shoulders moving quickly up and down, he seemed to be crying.

A few months later, at the end of winter, the three of us left for work.

Andrzej didn't take long to persuade, though I thought he'd be the most problematic, cos his sister was showing by that point. I had a feeling he'd be afraid to leave her, but when I told him, he agreed right away. We were standing in front of the shop, I remember that – he only thought about it for a moment, I wonder now what was going through his head, cos he looked at me and smiled, which rarely happened. If I could ask him anything, it wouldn't be what he was thinking as he prepared for death, but what it was that he pictured that winter when he said cheerily: "I'm going."

Pilot didn't care about anything by then, when he'd found out the girl was getting married, he'd vanished, he just sat beside the pond, he never stopped by the shop, he drank himself into a stupor and didn't want to take any work. Sometimes, Andrzej and I would carry him home – he was as light as a feather, getting thinner all the time and starting to turn yellow. That day, we put him in the car, we thought that he'd do a bit of work in the forest, get a change of scenery, that he'd forget, but after a month he was back, and two weeks later they fished him out of the pond.

Did he drown while under the influence? Or maybe he walked out on the thin ice on purpose? I don't know. I reckon he just got off the plane and wanted to check out what it was like underwater, that's what I tell myself – that maybe he wanted to be a diver instead of a pilot?

I didn't go to the funeral, Andrzej didn't bring it up either, I thought he'd say something, but no. Maybe I'd have found it easier to go with him, but we'd kind of grown apart by then, something was eating me up inside too, everyone had their own stuff going on. I remember when it came to the day and the hour that they were putting Pilot in the grave, I turned up the car radio as loud as it would go, so I wouldn't hear that fucking silence.

Not long after, I got in the orange Maluch and never looked back. The pond's completely overgrown now, someone filled in the hole he left, you can go there and see – they tarmacked the upper road, there's too many cars for the kids to go sledging, but the water's still sloshing where Pilot dug his pond.

The Little Bell

The room is big and dark. An old woman sits in an armchair, and next to her, in a less comfortable chair, is a little girl. The television's blue glow illuminates their faces. There are reading glasses on the table, a newspaper with the week's TV listings, pills in a plastic basket and information leaflets with dosage instructions scattered around. In the middle of the table are ammonia biscuits sprinkled with sugar, and tea with lemon, now cooled to room temperature. With each bite, the old woman draws up her hand in a scooping shape beneath her chin so as not to drop crumbs, and then offers her hand to the dog to lick. Pepper is seventeen years old and completely deaf and blind. Every time the woman sits down in the armchair, he jumps up on her lap and lays along her right-hand side, and when she tries to move him or shoo him away, he growls and bares his toothless gums. The little girl is wearing a colourful knitted jumper, pale purple leggings and sheepskin slippers, and her long, blonde plaits hang down her shoulders.

She goes over to the window. The house is on a hill and she can see the lights of the nearby town.

"When will Mum be here?" she asks quietly.

"I don't know yet. Come on, watch the film," replies Grandma.

The little girl obediently returns to her place. Hunched over slightly, she stares at the screen. She sees a woman with curly ginger hair, her face in her hands, crying, while a man hurriedly packs a suitcase and tries to fasten his tie. The woman has very long, crimson fingernails and she's shivering as if she's cold.

"It's because she's crying," explains Grandma. "When a person sobs, it's like they're ill, they shake. But you don't need to know that yet."

Tears come to the girl's eyes. She goes over to the window again, the red lights in the distance flicker on and off. It reminds her of a Christmas tree with flashing fairy lights, and the moon is like the star that her mother hangs at the very top. Maybe she's there somewhere amongst the lights and she'll be back any minute – or maybe that flashing one is her? The girl sits back down. Grandma wipes tears from her cheeks. The woman in the film is lying in a narrow coffin, her lips painted cherry red. To the side there is a small coffin and a photo of a smiling baby in the bath. The girl looks down at her slippers and swings her legs. My legs are like a merry-go-round, they can't stop turning, she thinks.

"It always ends this way," says Grandma. "You wind up alone and no one even asks if you got up in the morning, or what your favourite colour is. You'll see one day."

The girl doesn't reply. She uses a pen to black out the teeth of an actress on the front page of the newspaper, although she knows it will annoy Grandma.

"Dorotka, would you like to have black teeth like that?" asks Grandma. "No one would want you. Right, time for bed."

Dorotka goes over to the armchair where the dog is lying and lays her head gently on his back. Pepper grunts and breathes heavily. His coat is still shiny, but his body isn't as warm as it used to be. Since he's got old, the very moment he sits down somewhere soft, he rolls onto his side and falls asleep. Dorotka lifts and kisses each of his paws. She looks around the room, the light's already off. Shadows move across the furniture, floor and walls. She spins on her heels, trying to capture the dance.

"Come on, it's time!" calls Grandma from behind the door.

She's kneeling with her elbows on the bed, her lips moving rapidly, the occasional word audible. Dorotka kneels next to her and tries to copy her; her lips move noiselessly.

"Hear our weeping," says Grandma suddenly in a voice so loud the girl jumps with fright. "Look upon this child, who kneels before you and with a heart full of remorse, but also hope, asks for support and mercy. For her sake, redeem all our sins," she beseeches. After a pause, she adds conspiratorially: "That's how you talk to God, out loud. God likes it when you address Him with feeling and humility. Remember that." She looks Dorotka straight in the eyes.

"Does he know when Mum's coming?" asks the girl quietly.

"He knows everything," says Grandma with certainty.

"Then he should tell us, right now!"

"You won't get anywhere with anger. Everyone thinks they can ask God for something and he'll give it right away. I've never been given a thing, and I kneel at this bed every morning and night."

The bedding smells of washing powder, it's clean and stiff. Next to the bed, Grandma has a lamp and a magazine rack with copies of Domestic Guide, Housewife and You Time. She always reads for at least half an hour before bed.

"Look, it's Miss Poland, she was born just down the road from here, and now she's world-famous. Would you like to be like her?"

The girl shakes her head and is pleased to notice Miss Poland's toothy grin; tomorrow she plans to fill in two canines and a lower incisor.

"You keep your hands off my things! This is a souvenir. The people in the magazines know perfectly well what you do to them, and the people on TV too. One evil look and they'll tell the whole of Poland that Dorotka from Binarowa has rotten teeth or does stinky farts," says Grandma in a serious voice. "Me, I'd like to be that famous," she continues out of the blue. "I'd fix up the porch, because the door's broken and there's a draught in winter. I'd paint all the rooms and buy new shoes and a sheepskin coat. All my clothes are worn out." Grandma grabs at her nightgown and stretches it out in front of her. "Looks like it's hanging off a corpse, don't you think? That's how it always looks on the departed, every single one. And since I'm still alive, I want to look it. That side where you sleep is where I used to sleep, and your grandfather slept on the side where I am now. Don't you want to know why that was? He'd get up in the morning for work and, so as not to wake me, he'd be on the outside. But in fact, I was the one who got up first, I'd silently slide to the bottom of the bed and go and make coffee and sandwiches, usually with soft cheese. And I thought that all my life I'd be doing that in the morning, slowly, slowly shifting down the bed." Grandma picks up another magazine and flips through it carefully. "Now, time for you to turn around and go to sleep."

Dorotka lies down on her left-hand side, but she doesn't

close her eyes. She remembers a morning when she was woken by soft music from the radio. A man was singing in a high voice and a woman was making low-pitched, guttural sounds. She listened to the daily hustle and bustle, the closing and opening of cupboards, the fridge door creaking, dishes filling with water. Grandma moved quickly and quietly. Morning light flooded the room, making it impossible to get back to sleep. Dorotka lay with her eyes wide open; suddenly, all sounds subsided. She went to the door to peek through the keyhole. Grandma was sitting bolt upright, a cup of cocoa in front of her, both hands on the table. She was as still as a stuffed animal.

"Are you asleep?" Grandma asks suddenly. "Really, I took it very hard when your grandfather died. It was worst at night because his place in the bed was cold. That's when I moved to this side. At first, I'd lay a bit on one side, a bit on the other, I wanted to warm each part, and when one of them got cold, I'd quickly move over. All night long, left, right, left. I always thought the human body left its heat behind for longer, but then I found out that it doesn't. Have I told you what I was doing when they came to say that Józek wasn't coming back? I was lacing up his new shoes, and I just kept going, can you imagine? And he'd been so insistent a few days earlier that we shouldn't buy them! Maybe if he'd known that he wouldn't be wearing out those soles on the soft paths of our Lord Jesus Christ, he wouldn't have been so angry? Has anyone ever told you what to put in the coffin for the deceased? Remember this, it's best to have a watch so they can measure the time until we meet; and to prevent that time from dragging, you can put in a pack of cigarettes, for smokers, or playing cards, if they weren't the type to squander all their fortune. There's no point goading the dead once they're on the other side. And it's good to have a little bell, so that we can find them in the dark, because we never know if we mightn't end up searching for them at night. You can also include a photo of you together, because it's easy to forget over the years what your husband or wife looked like, even if they say: 'I'll never forget you,' that only applies on earth, things are different in heaven. There, people are like smoke and when you touch someone, you can walk through them or change their shape." Grandma lowers her voice, reaches out her hand and pretends to blow away some invisible dust. "You try it too," she says.

The girl raises her hands and wiggles her fingers.

"Dorotka!" Grandma interrupts her suddenly. "Careful not to tickle them. You can irritate the dead, just like the living."

Grandma places her hands motionless on the quilt and falls silent, and Dorotka clenches her eyes shut for a few seconds, then opens them again, because she would like to see someone dead one of these days, but the only one she remembers is her great-grandmother Stefania. It wasn't long ago that Great-grandma was still sitting hunched over on a large wooden bed in the corner of the kitchen, her head jerking this way and that. She was like the red hens that the children ran away from in the yard. The place where her bed had stood was always dark, and the kitchen was cool and large.

"Aren't you going to say hello?" her mother would ask, gently pushing Dorotka forwards.

A dry, trembling hand would emerge from the semi-darkness, trying to stroke her head, but instead landing on her cheeks, her forehead, or in mid-air. Dorotka would count to ten, turn around, and only then open her eyes. On the day of the funeral, the sun remained hidden, the cold, damp air quickly penetrated coats and chilled bodies, and the rain left small drops on their eyelashes. Dorotka walked close to her mother and tried to listen out for her great-grandmother jerking her head inside the coffin. It was quiet at the grave.

"Would you cry, child, if your mother or your uncle died?" Grandma turns and looks at her attentively. "Because at first, when I found out that Józek wasn't coming back, I couldn't say a word. I kept on lacing up his shoes, slower than usual, hole by hole, hole by hole, as if it would make time go backwards, make the film rewind, Jurek and Halina walking backwards, leaving the house with their faces towards me, through the orchard, then across the Pabisz family's field, they'd sit at the table, sip by sip, coffee filling their cups again, sip by sip, and in their house the phone would never ring and no one would say: 'Józek's dead.' I heard, I swear to you, I heard, though all the doors and windows were shut, your mother's long, high-pitched cry as she went to the orchard, when she found out that her father, your grandfather, was dead. And then, I swear to you, all the dogs started singing along, and I just stood there, I couldn't move. At night I dream of that cry, that howling in the dark, when I want to run but I can't even raise my arm. The worst thing is that it suddenly goes quiet, but then it erupts again, louder and louder. Your mother was crying for all of us, that's what I think now, so I wonder if you also have something like that inside you, if you're the kind to take everything to heart, even if it turns your heart black like the last piece of wood in a dying fire. What do you think?" asks Grandma and looks at Dorotka expectantly.

The girl shrugs and turns her gaze to the window, the lights of the town still visible below.

"I don't know, Grandma," she replies after a while.

"Your mother and uncle took my arms at the funeral," Grandma continues. "They led me all the way to cemetery hill." Grandma raises her arms to demonstrate. "Look, they were practically lifting me off the ground, I felt like I weighed nothing. But now let's sleep, and may we dream of nothing."

Dorotka wakes first. Grandma is lying with her back turned to her. The first rays of the morning sun are spilling into the room, creating stripes and blotches on the carpet. Dorotka would like to stay in bed and gaze at them, but she remembers that the dog always needs to be let out into the garden in the morning. She shifts slowly down the bed and quietly opens the door.

"Pepper, Pepper, time to pee," she whispers.

The dog is lying curled up in a ball, gasping for air and exhaling it quickly, as if he knew he couldn't pause. She calls him again, but only when she touches him does the dog raise his head, and he seems to be looking sideways with his distracted, blind eyes. The slack skin on his forehead tightens momentarily, forming a series of hairless wrinkles, but as Dorotka strokes him, the skin relaxes, the dog melts downwards and wants to go back to sleep. As Dorotka crouches down, about to pick him up, the dog snaps his toothless muzzle, but misses her hand. Dorotka pulls away and gives him a flick on the ear.

"Serves you right, you little shit," she says, giggling at the swear word.

The dog slowly gets to his feet and follows the girl.

"Are you going to listen to your mistress now? Because if not, you'll be sorry," she says, echoing the lines from yesterday's film.

It's a crisp morning. Dorotka sits on the low steps in front of the house and watches as the dog raises his back leg with difficulty and urinates on a rosebush. She stands up and raises her left leg to the side too.

"Watch how it's done, captain!" She runs to the dog and kisses him on the ear where she flicked him. "We'll sit together, you won't get away now, I'm keeping an eye on you, little one," she recites without faltering. She picks up the dog and settles him next to her on the steps. "Do you know when Mum will be here?" she asks quietly. "I followed her once in my pyjamas, but don't tell anyone."

She remembers the night she went outside to call to her mother. There was an old fluorescent lamp in the cowshed, which went out every few minutes. Dorotka had stared into the darkness for a long time, waiting for some movement, a shadow to confirm that her mother was there. Suddenly, a familiar figure had emerged from the blackness and placed a milk churn in front of her. Her clothes smelled of the cold, as if she'd returned from the dead.

"If you don't know anything about Mum, I'll ask someone else. Don't you go anywhere, I'm not finished with you yet."

Grandma's room was still in semi-darkness. She's asleep, she hasn't turned onto her other side or her back, like she tends to, thinks the girl. She stands in front of her grandma and asks almost inaudibly: "When will Mum be here? Tell me, please tell me. I'll be back in fifteen minutes, and if you're not ready for breakfast, you'll be sorry. What's all this? Still in your pyjamas, when the sun's already shining! Get a wriggle on!" she says, raising her voice. She looks around the room and finds the magazine with Miss Poland's face on it. She tries to put the letters together. "It says 'eh-vah'. Ewa," she says to her grandma. After a few minutes, Dorotka goes over and holds out the magazine to show how she's blacked out the woman's teeth. "You got what was coming to you. Go pig out and throw up," she adds plaintively.

Pepper nuzzles at her leg.

"Grandma's still asleep. Come on, I'll give you a sausage," she says to the dog.

She takes a ring of sausage from the fridge, along with some margarine and soft cheese, and bread wrapped in newspaper from the pantry. In the cupboard, she finds the bread knife that Grandma always uses. She throws bits of sausage on the floor and Pepper springs to life, sniffing around trying to track them down. The girl spreads margarine on the slices of bread, arranges the pieces of sausage neatly, and piles soft cheese on top. She pours water and too much raspberry cordial into a glass, the drink is thick with sticky droplets running down the sides of the glass. I'll take it in to Grandma, she'll smell it and wake up, Dorotka thinks.

"Sausage and cheese for you, Grandma, fresh from the pig and the cow." She pushes the plate under Grandma's nose and puts the glass to her lips. "Drink, come on, drink, or you'll dry up, you'll turn to sawdust and they'll throw you on the fire for kindling," she says. With a cloth, she wipes Grandma's mouth and the drops of drink spilled on her nightgown. "Fine, then. You'll see, your belly will swell up with hunger like the children on TV and then you'll be begging for it. But I'll pretend I can't hear you," she adds, and leaves.

The house always provided shelter from the heat, especially the large, dark kitchen. The low-set window overlooked the small orchard where a few crabapple and plum trees grew, and the raspberry bushes produced lots of fruit each year. Grandma made them into cordial. The girl stands in front of the kitchen window and for a moment, she thinks she sees Grandma's blonde hair among the tall, dense raspberry bushes. Barefooted, shoving past the dog on the steps, she runs towards the orchard.

"Grandma, Grandma! I saw you, don't hide from me!" she shouts tearfully.

She walks right into the middle of the bushes, turns around a few times, hears a rustling that grows louder and louder.

"Grandma, is that you?" she asks hopefully.

Pepper sidles towards her, raises his head and barks a few times, waiting for confirmation that it's really her. Dorotka leans over and hugs him tight. She finds raspberry leaves in his fur, dried corn stalks, and a wriggling caterpillar. Gathering all her courage, she picks a piece of tall grass and, with her eyes almost closed, knocks the caterpillar from Pepper's coat.

"Best friends forever," she says to the dog, who's squirming nervously as if he's forgotten how he got there.

Dorotka stares at the town in the distance. The hot air makes her vision blurry and she rubs her eyes. I've not been crying, but I can barely see, she thinks. It's so quiet that she puts her hands over her ears just to hear the hum.

"I get scared if I can't hear anything," she says to the dog and covers his ears too.

It's late in the afternoon when she comes out in front of the house again. The heat has subsided faster than it did the previous days. She looks at the orchard and imagines her mother crying, then imitates the dogs' howls.

"Owwwww, owwwww, owwwww," she wails, louder and louder each time until it scratches her throat.

The sound of a little bell rings out from the house, the kind that people attach to cats so that the birds can fly away in time. Grandma's calling me, she thinks. Maybe I didn't give her enough blankets? She quickly runs her hand over the back of the dog sleeping at her side, goes into the hall, opens the bedroom door and sees several dead flies floating in the glass of cordial, and a wasp, still alive. Quietly, she slides into bed and presses herself as hard as she can against Grandma's back. She drifts off to sleep. In the night, she hears the scraping of a key in the front door. Mum's back, she thinks. The little bell keeps ringing.

Hanna

When it's as hot as it is now, you want to be alone, so that no other body is clinging or standing nearby. You can sit upright and you needn't speak a word to anyone. And when I sit like that, looking out, I don't have to close my eyes to see the two of you. You're kneeling under an apple tree, sorting through the fruit. You put the wormy ones in a sack, and the fragrant, healthy ones on the sheets spread out in front of you. Your hands quickly separate the edible from the inedible. Not a sighting, not a peep, something's stirring while you sleep, maybe it's coming for you today, or might it get lost along the way, little girl, watch what you say. I can hear it clearly, Maria's voice carries down the hall, into the kitchen and straight to my ear. Maria is twelve again, with dark eyes and a voice that trembles as if she's about to cry. Maria is singing. Zofia spits out a wormy plum, grimaces and holds up a fat white worm. She lets it sit on her finger for a moment before throwing it onto the grass, taking off her shoe and trampling it with her bare foot.

"You come from the ground, so in the ground you go," she says.

She always says that when an insect, animal or human dies. Where are you now, my two little sisters? Are you walking side by side, or has one of you quickened your pace to catch up with me? And I'm sitting here, my hands numb from stretching them out in front of me. If only you could grab them, hold them tight, I'd bring you back. I can't sleep at night, it seems to me that someone's bustling around the kitchen, moving pots and humming to themselves. Bean, whose fur has bunched up into one big tangle, yaps constantly and keeps me awake. So I get up and look out of the window, but you're not there. What are you barking at, skinny little Bean, if you can't see my sisters? During the day, all I do is watch you in the garden, but I don't speak to you anymore, because no matter how loud I call, you don't hear me. This house has been so quiet for such a long time that sometimes I feel like I'm already in my grave. It's been so long since the cows mooed, they have different owners, the hens are cleaning their feathers in different dust. Your laughter is over on the other side, though it stills rings out. Maria, you used to say that I couldn't be on my own for even a minute. If you were to come in now and watch me sitting, how hard it is for me to get up, put on my tights and shoes, maybe you'd change your mind. But through this window I can see everything, I don't have to go out anymore. Besides, if I just got up and started walking, where would I go on these thin old legs with their baggy skin? Ever since I was a child, I've seen myself in the grave, I've just made the coffin bigger over time. One time I lay with a large cross on my chest, so big that it obscured my face, other times I had a devotional medal on my lips, or I lay on my stomach so as not to look anyone in the eye. The living want the dead to look at them, though the first thing they do is close their eyes.

It's quiet, only a fly hovering over the soft cheese, which I'm about to cover with a cloth. You'd like a snack too, little black fly. And what about the shit you've been walking on? Or the dog whose insides you've been guzzling after it suddenly collapsed by its kennel, thinking at the last moment that someone was stroking its back or calling its name? Just like death, you don't distinguish animals from people, savoury from sweet, you don't recognise colours, you don't remember names. You come as you please and every heart, liver and eye not yet closed belongs to you. The sky is steel grey today, the heat is slowly lifting, so I'll sit and watch. Everything here is blooming as always, hollyhocks, nasturtiums and rose bushes, as if the summer hadn't passed, the frost hadn't frozen the trees, the voles hadn't nibbled at the roots. Everything stands still, turning red and yellow. The bees, as usual, are working hard, the apples are turning red, and the plum moths are boring tunnels in the fruit, although there's no telling whether they will ever grow grey wings with dark spots and stretch them out in the heat of the early afternoon.

That morning, when I left the house, everyone was asleep. The sun wasn't lighting the road, people were hidden away in their bedrooms, barns and stables. Some were covered with a freshly aired eiderdown, others with straw and an old, threadbare blanket. I'd lain awake for a while, still hot and sweaty. Father was on the sofa in the kitchen, clutching at his duvet like he was hugging someone, and my sisters were in the bedroom, hand in hand. They'd slept in the same bed since they were little, and so it remained. I waited, wanting to breathe in the air they were exhaling. It was heavy, like tar that sticks to your shoes, that you carry around with you until it's worn away by stones and water. What were you dreaming after my dreams were over? Father – that he was walking behind Mother's coffin, holding Zofia's hand. She was carrying a bunch of poppies that she'd picked herself the day before. She was gripping so tightly that the flowers wilted, and she shook them like you would a stillborn kitten. The horse dragged Mother's coffin faster and faster through Binarowa and up the hill to Rożnowice. In his dream, Father was running behind the coffin, he let go of Zofia's hand, she fell over and started crying, but when he went back for her, there was no one there.

"I went back for Zofia, but she wasn't there, you can believe me or not," he repeated. "Off to the side I saw a burning haystack, butterflies spilling out of it, and when I turned around, Maria was running towards me, but instead of a head she had huge antlers. Then the cart with the coffin appeared again in front of my eyes, so I ran after it, I looked to see if the rest of you were running in that direction, and when it arrived, several days and nights passed one after the other. First, the sun was so hot that sweat poured down my back, and the next moment, it started snowing. And no one was there, the priest, the gravedigger, the neighbours, or you. The grave was undug."

My father had had this dream many times, and whenever we passed a haystack, he told us to look out for butterflies. That morning, I lay watching him from a distance, motionless on the narrow sofa in the corner of the kitchen. I believed in his fire quickly spreading to the hay, and little Zofia in her dirty tights, as she quietly said to the poppies: "Wake up, wake up, you've lain in the dark, silent earth long enough."

I knew that my sisters' dreams were still mellow, the two of them were swimming there, their hands freezing cold and they didn't want to come out, although I was calling to them louder and louder. My calls suddenly turned to song, and they sailed away to places they'd never heard of. Finally, I got up quietly, I wanted to kiss my father on the lips, but I knew that if I leaned over him, I would catch fire. Many time I've said goodbye to him, but I've never turned around, because if I'd looked, I'd have run to him. I put a grey dress on my sweat-drenched body, brown boots on my feet, and five heavy stones in my pockets.

What was I thinking then, when there was no turning back? No one has ever asked me that, though I know everyone's thought it. Making a pact with yourself is worse than with the devil, because then there's nowhere to hide; every corner is illuminated with bright light. Around here, people don't just disappear – it's rare someone opts for a beam and a rope, more often it's a gradual demise. They're not consumed by sorrow in a single moment, but throughout their lives, little by little, until suddenly they have nothing to breathe, they collapse, and for a while, it's "He died, pity", or sometimes not even that – everyone goes home, waving goodbye, until the next grave is dug. My memory fails me sometimes, I don't know who's still alive and who's dead. I was in the big city, not many people made it, the farthest my sisters got was the market nine miles away, "There's nothing worth going for", that's what we were always told, but I didn't want to stay in the city, I was drawn back. No one could understand it, some looked at me with envy, others laughed. What was the point? Go away to study, and come back to stare at cow rumps? Who would understand that even now, though I can barely stand, I have to open the window every day and feel the cold of the approaching night, because when it falls on me, I will close my eyes with no regrets? Ever since I was a child, when darkness came and the cold crept in, rather than putting on a jumper, I would walk around bare-skinned to absorb it all. I'd stand and watch as the fire-pinks and oranges faded slowly on the horizon and darkness fell. I would close my eyes, and each time hope that the world would be extinguished, as if someone had suddenly turned off the lights in all the houses, taken away the moon, sun and stars; that's my earliest memory. That morning, when there was no turning back, I thought about the relief of closing your eyes just once. Those who have long held hands with death cannot have those hands cut off. Let them go away, let it grow quiet, that's what I always thought.

I knew where it was deepest; we'd bathed in the river since we were young, Father taught us how to swim. Zofia was always the best, but she was never afraid of anything, if you told her to jump down a well or put her hand in a beehive, she'd do it without hesitation. But that day, I was the one who couldn't stop myself. I plunged into the river and then walked straight ahead, as if someone I loved very much was waiting on the other bank, and their life depended on whether I reached them or not. I only began to feel the stones in my pockets when the water reached my waist, they gave me courage, my feet moved with more certainty along the muddy riverbed. I heard nothing but the rush of the current, and I knew that when it got so quiet that you could hear every step, the rustle of clothes, it wasn't necessarily the calm before the storm. It was always either that someone was dying or they were already resigned to the idea. I've seen three deaths and none of them were alike. But how could death be similar if people are different? To each as he or she deserves or chooses. Some people, before they enter the barn, look at the sky for a moment, then at their own hands, as if they could put a halt to it, but these are the very same hands that are already reaching for the belt, the highest beam. Their life doesn't flash before their eyes, they don't suddenly start to cry. The eyes see only what's in front of them: hay, a bird cleaning its feathers, dust floating in the light. It grows dark for the dead and quiet for the living.

Now no one talks about that day, those who knew died long ago or their memories have failed, as mine sometimes does. Who'd have thought that a bucket of water spilled from these lungs with which I take in air every day? I was never ashamed of it, I just resented the man for pulling me out, he shouldn't have followed me. And what did I see in that final moment? Only what was there: the stony shore, the white poplars, their fragile upper branches tossed in all directions by the wind, the slowly breaking dawn, the promise of a new day.

Goodbye, It's Over

Who loves me, who respects me, who doesn't give a shit? I travelled over hills, through valleys, fields and forests to get one last look at him. But you look without seeing the whole person, only the eyes, whether they're misty, tear-filled, or calmly studying a beetle scurrying past a shoe. When that brown beetle with its gold-plated shell runs away fast enough to kick up dust or cause a sandstorm, it's tempting to raise that shoe and stop it. Just raise a foot in its old, battered shoe and stamp it down with full force. But when you see those eyes in front of you, behind a mist, as if they'd just woken up or been crying, you can't bring yourself to say the words: "Goodbye, it's over, it was nothing." You stand and look, and you think to yourself: I'll remember all this forever. But later, you just know that it was winter, the dry branches were sagging under the snow and so black that you might think they'd been specially burnt just for this moment. Even in dreams, where the image sometimes returns, it's only black and white, one little leaf swaying in the wind, but when you close and open your eyes again, even that's gone.

"But I've lived here all my life," says Henia and turns around. "I could count the number of new houses on one hand. So it ain't that easy meeting people here. The house on the hill, see it? There, where that big brick one is at the top, and a bit further down, the one covered with roofing felt, well, I got my first glimpse of the world in the one below that. But what kind of glimpse was it? When babies are born, they're as blind as cats or they see everything black. When my Dorotka was born four years ago, she had such big, deep blue eyes, it scared me, when I stared at her for a long time, it seemed like she wasn't looking at me, but at something behind me. Plenty of times I turned around quick so it wouldn't get away, but I never managed to catch it. What I think, though I don't tell no one, is that we should feel the least sorry when little babies die, cos they've got one foot here and one foot there. It's common sense, if you've been in the depths, in darkness for so long, and human voices can barely reach you, then when you enter a new world, you don't belong to it right away. It's like when you wake up and you don't know if you're holding hands with a living person or a corpse. That's what I think sometimes. Maybe others think the same? Should I tell you something about my daughter? Well, she didn't come from the kind of love I'd have liked, that I dreamed of at night and didn't want to wake up. But that's all I'll say about that. When I close my eyes, I see something different."

It's summer, early afternoon. Henia stands in front of the house, hands on her hips. She's holding a wet rag in her left hand. Her fingers are short, her nails bitten, and she clenches her fists until her fingertips turn white. Her dark, unwashed hair falls over her eyes and halfway down her neck. Her large breasts bulge in her tight blouse, and her knee-length brown skirt exposes her swollen legs. Henia stares out in front of her and smiles. She has strong, healthy teeth the colour of pale river stones. Every now and then she raises her hand and waves the rag to her daughter and the neighbours' children playing at the crossroads. A large puddle has formed there, and a few ducks are slowly circling. The children bring pieces of coloured glass up to their eyes and look through them at the sinking sun. Dust from the gravel road rises high above their heads. Will it be this hazy when I die, too? Henia wonders, bending now. Then she takes a piece of red glass from the ground and looks at the sun too. After a moment, the glass still to her eye, she turns her gaze to the neighbour's large, well-kept house. To me it's red, to someone else it's green, each of us sees something different, she thinks.

"Well, I get on fine with everyone here," she continues, not taking the glass away from her eye. "The ones from the middle house, with the roofing felt, treat my Dorotka as their own. She gets food there, she can take a leak, they dress her, even wash her. I swear to God, they do so much for her, sometimes I feel ashamed, cos I'm her mother after all. They've got two kids, a boy and a girl, she's almost Dorotka's age, one month apart. I remember our bellies were growing at the same pace, but even there, things are messed up. The older boy has a different father, and even with the little one, it was hit and miss if she'd be accepted. I remember it well, we walked hunched over so people wouldn't know from looking at us. But who am I to talk about women's issues? What's between someone's legs, that's their business. Now, what about the militiaman's house, though since they've done away with the militia, he wants everyone to call him a policeman instead! Brick, with foundations," Henia suddenly comes to life. "Everything's so smart there, linoleum and a bathroom, and pictures of Jesus and Mary hanging on the wood panelling, and others too, anything you could imagine: chrysanthemums, a red rose, a stork on one leg. Beautiful, like they'd been glued on, not painted from someone's head. At ours, we always slept in the two main rooms and the kitchen, and there was thirteen of us including our parents. Now we've got a bit of luxury too, cos it's just me, Dorotka, Mum and Andrzej, when he ain't away working or wherever, the others have gone off into the world and the sky. There, at the neighbours', everyone always had their own room, two of them sharing at most. But once a militiaman, always a militiaman, the house has to be spick and span.

"Have I been there much? Three times I've been inside, cos everything's all done up, you don't go in with your shoes on, you leave them out front. Anyone brought in mud or dust and Pan Władek would call them over and make them clean it up on their hands and knees, no mercy. Once I went when all my waters had drained and I needed to call an ambulance, the second time when I was helping the priest with his house calls, cos it was slippery, and I only looked in from the porch, and the third time was when my brother Andrzej swallowed a load of pills. He'd do that every now and then, he got something in his head and started preparing for the other world. That time I ran, cos his eyes were clouding over, he'd stopped talking and started drooling. That was the only time I went in the room where the phone was, but Pan Władek didn't want to dial the number. 'It'll pass, like the shits,' he said, but it wasn't going to pass. When I got on my knees he gave in, but then my throat tightened."

Henia drops the piece of glass and stamps it into the

ground with the tip of her shoe. She puts her hands around her neck and her fingertips turn white again.

"Like someone was choking me," she says. "Only three times in my life I've felt like I couldn't swallow, like something was burning inside. One time was then, with Andrzej, when I ran to make the call, and the second time, after Dad died, I leaned against the apple tree and I couldn't stop crying." She breaks off and looks around. "We ain't got much here," she says, recovering suddenly. "The fire station on the hill, the school over the hill, the cemetery above the school, with the one German buried among our lot, cos he tilted his head to the left too late and got hit in the eye, there's the chapel, the burial mound from the Swedish Deluge, and that's it. Oh, and the cemetery in the woods, where they buried them ones who puked at first, and at the end their voices changed." Henia squeaks in imitation: "They had high-pitched voices so you couldn't tell if it was a bloke or a bird. Not everyone cares for jokes like that, but I like to have a sense of humour. Without it, they'd have carted me off a long time ago. Sure, you can't always have a grin on your face, but – and please don't tell no one – I laugh sometimes at funerals too. When I see a shrivelled-up corpse in her best dress, I know that under that stiff crêpe she's wearing her prettiest knickers that were hanging around in her wardrobe for a good thirty years. Not for her husband, but for death."

Henia pauses for a moment and waves to the children even more vigorously. A little girl with long, blonde hair is sitting in the road and refusing to get up. Two older boys pull her up by her arms and drag her over the stones. The little girl screams loudly.

"It's good the kids are there," Henia says with a smile. "I don't like it when things get so quiet that you can only hear a fly buzzing in a glass, or the leaves rustling when the wind picks up. This time of day, the sun shines different; if you watch, you can see people's shadows get longer, it's easy to spot, take a look sometime. They're meant to be our shadows, but I was always afraid of them, legs like stilts, a strange hump sticking out of me. Maybe that's really how I look, and I just wish it was different? I don't like looking at the road in late summer, I came out today cos I heard Mongrel yapping at the neighbours' place. He was banging his chain against the kennel so hard, like he was about to break lose and dart off somewhere. But where would he run to? Sometimes he breaks free, but he just wanders around, he doesn't know he could be wherever he wants. So today, for once, I came out and watched. No one knows that I was once standing like this, and he came along. It was exactly the same, but quiet, I don't like that. He came along and the sun shone brighter on him, probably cos it wanted me to see him better, but his shadow was even and straight. Who came along? Mirek, of course. Who else, for God's sake! He was beautiful, I ain't never seen no one like him since. Tall, with dark hair, eyes pale green like water in a clear river when the light hits it, so pretty. Now I can't even look at a river – when I pass one, my heart stops, then it beats so hard I can't take a breath. From fear, I guess, thinking I might see him up close again. When someone says they'd like to live their whole life a second time, I don't believe them. They're just saying that cos they're afraid that when they die, it'll turn out there's nothing there, or they'll end up in hell, smack in the middle of the fire. I don't know for sure, but I think if they chuck me into hell, they'll make me stand and watch, just like now, and Mirek will come along, then disappear, then come along again, and disappear again, forever."

Henia's standing in front of the house. It's a summer afternoon; her grey dress, wet with sweat, clings to her rounded belly. Milk is leaking from her engorged breasts, it's nearly time for a feed. Henia scratches at her sore, itchy nipple. And look at her, so skinny already, she thinks, seeing her neighbour from up the way. She watches as the neighbour quickly herds the sheep into the fold, then carries over a large block of salt and throws it to the animals. The woman notices Henia and raises her hand high in greeting. After a while she disappears, the door slams. The neighbour's dog emerges and tries to trace where the sound came from. He stiffens and tenses his back, then gives up and returns to his kennel, curling up in the shadows. It is quiet and empty. Everyone's hidden away, bellies exposed to the heavens after lunch, falling into shallow, fitful, dreamless naps. They awake hungry and sweaty, lie motionless and wish they never had to get up again. They swing their stiff legs over so their feet touch the floor, straighten their backs, and stare ahead, their eyes watery.

Henia watches a man coming along the road, shielding his face from the sun. Her eyes blaze like burning grass in autumn.

"How do, pretty lady!" the man says to Henia, and scans the farmyard. "I see it's all set up." He goes over to the smokehouse by the pigsty and taps the metal roofing a few times. "It'll smoke well. You'll eat your fill this winter."

Embarrassed, Henia tries to stretch her dress down and hide her big post-pregnancy belly. She folds her arms over her breasts, but before she can say anything, the man pipes up again.

"I'm Mirek. From Osobnica. I came into town on the last bus, then along Podwale Street to Binarowa, right to your door. Przepióra won't be slaughtering any more pigs, not for the next two weeks anyway. What, you don't know? They took him to the hospital in Gorlice, he turned all yellow, he's out of the game for now. They sent for me, the two of us learned the trade from our grandad, I'm sure I'm up to the task, don't worry yourself," says Mirek reassuringly. "And what's your name? Let me guess! Maria, perhaps?"

Henia shakes her head.

"Zofia, then?"

"No, sir," she replies, embarrassed. "My parents named me Henia."

"They couldn't have picked a more beautiful name! Early start tomorrow, I'll be here at seven. Have the kettle boiled and ready. Is there a man around to help me? A husband or relative?"

"No, no one. My brother Andrzej ain't home," says Henia quietly.

"He won't be back by tomorrow?" Mirek asks.

"He's gone to work in the woods, see," says Henia. "But I've done the pigs before with this guy Piotrek," she adds.

"The two of us will manage just fine, don't you worry. I'll go and say hi to my relatives now, spend the night there," he adds. "Or if not, then in the open air or in a barn. Maybe I'll dream of you."

Embarrassed, Henia follows the man with her eyes until he disappears over the hill past the fire station.

"Maybe I'll dream of you," she repeats and giggles. And then: "Mum! Mum!" Henia runs into the house, shouting. "Przepióra's sick, he ain't slaughtering the pig! They took him to the hospital in Gorlice! They've sent us some Mirek all the way from Osobnica, never seen him before."

"I've known all that since yesterday."

"Then why didn't you say?"

"I forgot. And what's the point of knowing who's going to knock an animal on the head? Does it make a jot of difference to you? They say this bloke Loopy makes the same sausages, plenty of salt and garlic. Know why they call him Loopy? Because he's got a screw loose," says the woman with a laugh, chewing on a piece of bacon rind. "A bit like you, eh?"

"Mum! Don't you dare tell him I can't write."

"Or read," her mother adds maliciously.

"Don't tell him," begs Henia.

"I won't say a word, I shan't be chattering with him in any case. Heńka, you'd better sew up that hole before tomorrow. We've already got one fatherless child here, I'll not be raising any more of you!"

"Give it a rest, Mum, I'm not interested in him."

Henia goes over to the cradle and picks up the baby, uncovers her breast and begins to feed. She rocks back and forth, back and forth, her eyes are closed.

"You don't need to be interested in him. All it takes is for him to be interested in you, even a little."

It's a foggy morning, the dog doesn't want to go out, even when Henia holds out a piece of bread for him to sniff.

"Pepper! You ill or what?" she says to the dog. "Come on," she encourages him, "come on." The dog stares at her, then curls up in a ball and closes his eyes. "Someone wants to sleep some more, eh, you stinky lazybones," she says, amused. "You'll soon come running when you catch a whiff of blood and guts."

She brings in some water in two buckets and puts the pots borrowed from their neighbours on a hot baking tray in the kitchen. Pan Władek wouldn't lend us a thing, but he'll come by for a sausage, she thinks. She sits outside the house and looks towards the fire station.

"Hold the rope tighter, or she'll get away! I already knocked her on the head once before you got here, but it only laid her out for a minute," Mirek shouts impatiently. "First time I've slaughtered a pig with a woman," he adds more gently and winks at Henia. They've kept her too long, he thinks, overgrown as fuck, they'd better not complain when there's more fat than meat.

The pigsty is cramped and there are no windows. The animal wasn't fed that morning, Mirek has tossed the bucket into the corner. The pig is moving from one side of the sty to the other, generally heading towards the door, but as her fear grows, her movements become increasingly erratic. Henia has the feeling that the pig recognises her voice, so she stops and falls silent. Then she grabs the rope hard and digs her heels into the earth. The small, brown eyes stare at her, and a moment later, a high, drawn out squeal escapes from the animal's mouth. She's calling me, thinks Henia. Mirek is shifting from one foot to the other, as if he's about to take Henia by the arm and start dancing with her. He picks up the axe, takes a swing and strikes with all his might in the middle of the head. The animal goes into a fit of short convulsions, the body resembling a rubber ball that is thrown once and bounces several times on the ground.

"Done. She didn't put up much of a fight," says Mirek, pulling a knife from his belt. "Quick, hand me the bowl, we'll bleed her. Check if it's clear."

In a single motion, he slits the throat and feels the resistance of the fat.

"You did well," he says to Henia and touches the nape of her neck. "I always say not to let the animal out on the threshing floor, cos then it struggles more. It should be slaughtered in the place where it eats, shits and gives birth," he adds confidently.

"The stench of cooked meat and tripe always disgusted me, but there was no other way, that's what you did with a pig. It lingered in the house for a long time, kind of sweet, in your hair, on your clothes, you could smell it everywhere, even if you aired the place all day long. And everywhere greasy, sticky, bare feet splashing with every step. When I was little, I dodged it, I went out behind the house or into the valley, so I didn't have to hold the basins for the butchers or slice the garlic. I just walked, and I was gone. Of course, I always looked forward to the smoked sausage, I liked it with plenty of salt and pepper, lots of garlic, not too greasy, so that when you cut it, it came out in nice, even, dense slices. But that day, when Mirek was cutting up the pig, the smell didn't bother me, I wanted the day not to end, or to end and start again the same. So that I could sit in front of the house and he'd come along.

"People round here will probably say different, but the truth is I didn't follow Mirek to Osobnica right away. There was almost nothing left of summer, autumn flew by, the first snow fell, Dorotka was already on regular milk. Mirek would come by sometimes, though the baby wasn't his, he even started getting used to it, but it was a long trip and the bus was expensive. Five złotys to Jasło one-way, four złotys to Osobnica, not much difference, and in Jasło you can buy everything: colourful dresses and skirts of different lengths – long, knee-length, mini – shoes with high or low heels, gold earrings and rings; most of it was imported. Finally, in winter, I just up and went, straight to the bus stop, only two buses went that way each day, so I took the earlier one, cos the journey was exactly fifty minutes, and I said to the driver: 'Osobnica, please.' I didn't take the baby. No, I left her with my old ma, nowhere else she'd have been better off, my heart had broken free and followed Mirek, so I had to go after it. Cos how could I live here without him? Would I have a black hole in my chest, so all my insides, every tiny little bone, would be on show? I didn't spend long walking around the village looking for Mirek, although I didn't know where his house was, he never told me, but when you're from round here, you know that people will tell you everything: where someone sleeps and where they wake up.

"So we're standing there in front of his house, he didn't ask me in, the dry branches bent under the weight of the snow, they were black, that's all I remember. His eyes weren't moist, that's for sure, I welled up, but I didn't shed a tear, I stood my ground, like that time with the pig. And he said: 'Goodbye, it's over, it was nothing, I don't give a shit,' and he pointed towards the bus stop. Maybe he didn't want a spinster with a kid, maybe he was ashamed, but when we met, he knew he wasn't getting me on my own, so who knows? I must have been waiting for the bus home for three hours, freezing cold, pacing back and forth. But then when I was riding home in the warmth, looking at the fields, at the people and houses, how they were decorated, I loved it. Mirek and I would paint our house lilac, and the roof red, I thought. I took my sandwich from the plastic bag and ate it, it had onion and pork fat in, delicious, but that last bite stuck in my throat, a strange lump, like only twice before and never again since."

The Cliff

It was a beautiful day like this, summer, you could walk around in just your underpants, no one was ashamed of anyone here, because there was nothing to hide. At the last judgment, everyone will be standing side by side, not a fig leaf in sight, just as they were born, which is to say in the body they died in, but naked, that's what I mean. Saturdays in the summer meant a trip to the Ropa river, which can be fast and deep, but that's what rivers are, right? Not splashing around in the shallows, but going in up to your neck, up to your head, disappearing under the water. You have to feel its weight, that sometimes it will bash you about a bit, and other times it will embrace you like love, and it grows pleasant, light, and then you can die. Otherwise there's no point. This is my earliest memory – my father and I are going to the river, we're making our way through the big butterbur leaves, I hold his hand tight and wish I could never let go, and then I go into the water, I lose my balance and fall beneath the surface, I can't catch my breath, I'm drowning, and it's not my father but my uncle who pulls me out, sits me up and tells me to cough. I think it was then that I sensed for the first time that my closest person wouldn't always be beside me, that I had to let go of that hand in advance. And then the second time, when I was hit by a car on a zebra crossing – bad luck, three other people were crossing with me, including my fiancée, and it only hit me, in the left leg, it still hurts sometimes. "I was blinded by the light," the driver explained. That was a beautiful summer's day too, I must have twisted my ankle in a strange way on impact, because the entire sole had come away from my left shoe. I sometimes wonder what the deal was with that light. What happened? Did I cease to exist to him for a few seconds? Because if he didn't see me, it's as if I wasn't there. If I'm wrong, feel free to correct me, I won't be offended. When I was sitting in the road, I hesitated for a moment, unsure whether I would ever get up again. And it wasn't my fiancée to whom I reached out my hand, but my friend. We do strange things sometimes, maybe I was already starting to understand that something can be missing or lost. But here I am going on about myself, and I was supposed to be talking about Małgorzata, please forgive me. This bright day brought it back to me, because when they found her, it was also summer, a real scorcher, and a strange brightness that you don't get every day. It's reminiscent of childhood, a rare experience, you get up in the morning, go for a walk and suddenly, for a moment, you see the world differently, the air is clearer and the sun gives off a muted yellow glow, it's quiet, you can hear all of nature, a passing fly, the swoosh of the tall alders, poplars and beeches, and even a fox prowling around in the bushes that stops, flummoxed by the sound of its own steps. It was a day like that, as I said, when they found Małgorzata.

But we need to go back twenty years.

*

Back when there were fewer cars, children could go sledging down from the market square, because the town, laid out on hilltops, stood high above the villages. From the town hall tower, where a twenty-four-hour clock marked the time of day, you could look down into the surrounding valleys. The smell of crude oil floated in the air, the pumpjacks in the earth-red excavations looked like hard-working animals. Day after day, their black heads would bob up and down. When women hugged their children at the end of the day, in their hair they would smell the pungent odour of bitumen mixed with the child's sweet scent, which most resembled candy floss. The combination of these two smells evoked another: that of burnt sugar. In the centre of town, there were rows of two-storey tenements, a synagogue among them, which now housed the library and the municipal offices. The closed hospital had fallen into disrepair; the walls were crumbling, there was no glass in the windows, and loved-up couples snuggled in corners as if they were locked in a room with the lights off. The river flowed below the town, past the ramparts, violent and deep in some places; many had been drawn into its whirlpools. Its dark blue-grey current was hypnotising, giving the impression that at the very bottom there could be a better life.

A different one than here, at least, Małgorzata thought, locking up at the bakery on the market square one late afternoon. As usual, she didn't get on her bike right away, but walked, the sun casting a muted glow on the paving slabs, people taking shelter in the coolness of their homes; everything seemed deserted and uninhabited. A dog with a ginger coat crossed her path and barked three times, then tucked its tail between its legs and quickly disappeared, someone waved to her from a red Syrena, the only car that passed her on her way home. Where's Wroński going at this time of day? she wondered. She turned around and the man honked twice. I shouldn't have looked, he'll get ideas, she thought, frightened. Wroński had never married; he was short, fifty years old, and had thick, curly hair that he was constantly running his fingers through. In the summer, he wore a straw hat and mesh sandals from which his yellowed toenails protruded. He ran the large Rainbow homewares shop near the bakery where Małgorzata worked, and he came in almost every day for a chat. He asked how business was going, how many sliced buns they'd sold, and how many dinner rolls, sometimes he said what was out of stock in his shop and that people look not at the quality but at the price, and a month later they come back complaining that the sorghum was falling out of their brooms.

"I'm always happy to advise. Whether you're choosing a sausage knife or a simple broom. Please keep it in mind, ladies," he always said before he left.

He was calling in at the bakery more often in the afternoons, because Małgorzata was alone there after three o'clock, when the other shop assistant finished her shift.

"He can't manage without you," said her colleague. "I wouldn't be so picky, the clock's ticking, and so what if there's a big age gap? That's okay, at least you can be sure he won't run off with some floozy. I'm telling you, no one will see you as young again, you have to take what you can get." And when she was having a bad day, she added: "You're no queen yourself, let's be honest."

"It's not that he's old, it's that he's short," Małgorzata would say and look away.

"It's not like you're a giant! There's no pleasing you. You'll regret it someday," said her colleague.

A week before, Wroński had come into the bakery for the last time. Małgorzata had noticed right away that he was acting strangely. He was avoiding eye contact and kept tapping his fingers on the counter.

"Come with me to Lake Rożnów this Sunday, I bet you've never been before," he said suddenly in a single out-breath. "I'll bring the provisions, of course, and there's no need to chip in for the petrol, it's far away, but we'll be back by evening, please don't worry yourself about that," he added more slowly and assertively.

"I've been there before. And I won't be going anywhere with you, not this Sunday, or any other day. Please don't come in here again, unless it's to buy something," she replied crossly.

Maybe I was too firm or too loud, maybe I should have been quieter, so as not to hurt him, she thinks now as she makes her way slowly down to the end of the market square. She's short, with a pronounced waistline. Her long, slightly wavy hair, which she usually wears loose so that it falls freely down her back, is the colour of ripe hazelnut shells and gleams with red highlights in the sun. She usually wears black midi dresses, fitted at the top and flared at the bottom, that's the style she likes the most, and she pairs them with wedges; she almost never wears makeup, sometimes just paints her lips the colour of raspberries. She is thirty-four and lives alone; her mother died the previous autumn, her father when she was in primary school. On her way, she passes her old school, the Deuce grocery shop, the butcher's below, and right on the corner, where the pavement narrows dangerously so that only one person can walk along it, a small watchmaker's shop. Małgorzata walks over to that side, leans her bicycle against the wall and looks at the display in the bookshop window, as she does every day. Nothing has changed there for months, but she still reads the book titles. She runs her fingers through her hair, turns sideways and looks at her reflection in the glass. Maybe if Father hadn't died, I'd have had time to read all those books, she thinks. They'd have sent me to university, far away; I'd come back to visit, go to the bakery, buy the best loaves and always half a challah for Sunday. And no Wroński would even dare look at me, except in secret, and certainly not speak to me. Then I'd start coming here with my fiancé, my parents would take to him straight away, he'd stay in the box room, where the window overlooks the orchard, no one would have anything to say.

It's only when she reaches the railway tracks that she gets on her bike and looks to the left. Near the station is the metal foundry cooperative where her father worked all his life, and before that, the sawmill. After the station, she crosses the bridge; whenever she and her father cycled that way, she would clasp his back even tighter for fear of the rushing water. She tried hard not to look down, imagining herself falling and slowly drowning, the current propelling her body like a log she had once seen there. So, as usual, she accelerates and feels slightly lightheaded; out of the corner of her eye she sees the blue railings flashing past rhythmically. I'm never going to school again, she'd thought when her father died. Only later had she felt sorry for herself; she'd gone into the box room and, staring out at the blossoming apple tree, cried in silence. Her father used to sit her on the pannier rack of his bicycle every morning and take her to school in the town he was from. She was the only child in Binarowa who attended the school in town.

"She'd better not turn into some sort of smart-arse!" her mother would joke spitefully.

Her father would drop Małgorzata right outside the school doors, and later, she'd wait in the locker room until he finished work and took her home. She doesn't remember the first day she went alone, but she remembers the days after that. Before the bridge, she would close her eyes and pedal as fast as she could, sometimes losing her balance and falling over. It was worst in spring because she'd ruin her tights and then have to listen to her mother yelling. On her way to school, she began looking more closely at nature; her father had taught her to recognise trees and birds. Most of all, she liked hearing the blackbird go from a low whistle to a high warble; she imagined it perched with ruffled feathers at the top of the tree as the other birds fell silent. Sometimes in the bushes by the river she heard the voice of a corncrake, which sounded like the creaking of the pantry door, and it made her laugh. It was worst in late autumn, she was afraid of the dusk and the pumpjacks, which in the deep blue light looked like hungry horses with no muscles, about to lunge at her with their toothless mouths.

With each passing year, Małgorzata missed her father more and more, although her mother had assured her that only the memory of the grief would remain.

"It passes more quickly for children. They forget in a flash," she had said.

The sorrow would hit her when she least expected it – right after waking, when her mother was bustling about in the kitchen and the light was bursting through the curtains, or when she was sitting with her friends by the river and everyone suddenly fell silent. Back then she didn't know how to control it, it would sweep over her body and she'd lose the strength in her arms and legs, barely managing to hold her smouldering cigarette. Even Staszek, whom she had been dating for several years, didn't notice it. They had known each other since they were little, and at the end of primary school, he'd started waiting for her after school and walking her home.

"He'll make a good husband and father," her mother had said when they reached eighteen. "Maybe you'll get married?"

But Małgorzata didn't reply.

She also remained silent when Staszek confessed his love to her, and when they were lying naked, she turned her head to avoid looking at him. It was the same with other men. All she wanted was touch, which eventually stopped giving her pleasure. And she remembers very clearly the day she gave Staszek the ring back. She ran fast, a storm was approaching, the sky darkened and the first drops were falling on the pavement. She wanted to get there before she was soaked through by the rain, she accidentally bumped into a man carrying a milk churn, a few drops stained her skirt.

"Bitch!" he shouted after her, but Małgorzata didn't even turn around.

Staszek was waiting on the bridge with an umbrella. Małgorzata yanked the loose pearl ring from her finger and placed it in her open palm.

"I don't want it," was all she said.

He pushed her hand, the ring fell onto the tarmac. He immediately picked it up and threw it in the river. Małgorzata watched its short flight and was relieved when it disappeared into the dark water. She saw Staszek often after that, but he stopped talking to her. She was glad that she would never hear his low, doleful voice again, except perhaps by chance, from a distance.

This willow has been growing here for as long as I can

remember, she thinks. This strange tree, stunted over the years, rotted from within; if you peer inside it, it looks like a straw-lined manger. She reaches the bend, another half a mile and she'll be home. The farther from the town, the fewer buildings and pumpjacks, the more meadows and knolls as placid as animals sedated by the heat. She climbs higher and higher, passing Pani Owczarowa's house. She sees Alicja's granddaughter: the girl is sitting on the steps, hugging the old dog and whispering something in its ear. She says hi, but the girl doesn't notice her.

She turns left, towards the orchard, though she should be going straight. I won't come back, she thinks.

During the holidays, the children usually want to go down to the river, or to the slag heaps, which are covered in delicate field horsetail. They rarely venture near the cliff, because there have been a few serious accidents there. There's even a sign: "No entry! Narrow paths and unstable ground." One sultry afternoon, Kuba, Weronika and Michał are walking lazily towards the bridge. Michał, the oldest, is marching on ahead, holding a slender hazel stick. Single blades of grass protrude from between the paving slabs, and Weronika deliberately treads on them. They hear the sound of a car crossing the bridge, but they don't look to see where it turns. They're busy staring at the raging current.

"The river's angry today," says Kuba, the youngest.

"Pissed off," replies Michał.

"You shouldn't say that," says Kuba.

"Why's that?"

"Someone might hear."

"Helloooo, anyone there? Hey, river, who ya hiding? There's no one here. Come on!"

"Where are we going?" asks Weronika.

"You don't question orders, you just obey them," says Michał bossily.

"Go on, tell me!" she pleads.

"Stop whining, come on."

The children walk slowly, tired from the heat of the long day. They pass the pumpjacks, the rotten willow, and make their way up the hill, where the paving slabs get wider and wider. Near the forest, they pass a hut, the ground around it strewn with rubbish, old mattresses, blankets and clothes. One of the windowpanes has been smashed by a branch and you can peer inside, the rest of the windows are covered. The sun is dipping, the colours slowly fading, coated at first in a muted yellow, then grey. "Shall we look inside?" asks Michał.

"Better not, someone might be sleeping in there and they'll be angry," says Weronika hesitantly.

"Then you stay, you'll never find out what's in there, and we won't tell you, no matter how much you beg us."

"What if someone's living there and they start chasing us?"

"Then we'll run to Pani Owczarowa's, she's the closest. Anyway, I've got a stick." The boy waves the hazel branch. "He'll get his arse kicked."

The children tiptoe towards the hut. Kuba drags an old box behind him, because he knows they won't be able to reach the window. They've tried to look inside many times before, but the dark, thick curtains blocked their view.

"Girls first," Weronika says quietly but firmly, narrowing her eyes because she thinks it makes her look more dangerous.

"You didn't want to go in just now! What if you see something and you scream or faint? I have to go first and then

I'll tell you if you can look," says Michał, pushing his way forwards.

Weronika raises her hands slightly and clenches her fists.

"Don't you dare!"

"Be quiet, silly! If someone's there, you'll wake them up. We'll look together, then, we can both fit, come on."

"Fine," she replies, satisfied. "And you, Kuba, stand there and check if anyone's coming." Kuba merely nods.

Inside the hut it's cleaner than they'd expected. There are folded blankets and two pillows on the bed. Someone has left tins of coffee and sugar on the table, and there's a tall jar half full of granulated tea. Next to it is an unwashed plate with fresh food scraps. In addition to the bed, there are two yellow plastic chairs. A shelf hangs on the wall at an alarming angle. Above the bed is a large painting of a dark-coated dog with a pheasant in its mouth, the eyes of the bird a dull white.

"What an ugly painting," says Weronika. "Pani Owczarowa has one like that in her porch, but the birds have their eyes closed, they're lying in front of the dog, and the dog's smiling with its ears pricked up."

"It's waiting to be stroked," replies Michał. "When dogs do something right, you have to stroke them on the head or pat them on the back," he explains with confidence and ruffles Weronika's hair.

"Get off, Mum will be angry that I messed up my plaits!"

Kuba is standing still and listening, focused and alert. Suddenly, he thinks he hears footsteps, like someone walking through a field of stubble. Because of the heat, the grass has dried out in many places and turned the colour of sand.

"Let's go!" Kuba yells with all his might and, without waiting for the others, he darts away.

Weronika and Michał soon catch up with him. They run

for a long time, and when they finally look up, they see the cliff, densely covered with trees. The roots of a poplar are exposed, scoured by the water, creeping down the slope. The tree looks like it's about to topple over.

"Come on!" Michał shouts, frightened. "We'll hide from him up there!"

The boy sits with his head lowered, drawing patterns with his fingers on the tabletop: circles, squares, six-pointed stars. He steals a look out of the window, a jay is bringing worms to its young. In anticipation of the next helping, the little birds' beaks are constantly open. The tree branches thrash against the panes, it's windy, the boy flinches every now and then when he hears a noise in the corridor. The draft keeps yanking a door open somewhere, then slamming it shut.

"You saw her first?" asks the policeman.

"Yes," replies Michał.

"What else do you remember?"

"Um, she was lying down, her arms were spread."

"So you were the first to see the body?"

"Pani Bielecka."

"Yes, the body."

"I dunno if it was a body. It was Pani Bielecka."

"How can you not know if it was a body? You're a body, I'm a body, Pani Małgorzata Bielecka is a body, and so's your mummy. You're in the second year of school. Can you read?"

"Yeah, I'm good at reading. The other day we had that one that goes: 'Four little foxes playing in the woods, one ran fast just to see if he could...'"

"Yeah, yeah, that's enough. You're good with nursery

rhymes, but not so hot at remembering facts. So she was lying there, and then what?"

"Nothing. I stared at her."

"From where?"

"From above. She stared at me too."

"What do you mean, she stared at you?"

"Her eyes were open."

"So she was alive?"

"Dunno."

"But did you get the sense she was alive? Maybe she moved her leg, her arm, her head?"

"No. She was just staring."

The boy swings his legs and looks around the room. Perched at another small table, a young policeman is holding a biro and gazing expectantly at the chief, waiting to be told what to write down. Behind the boy's back, the wall is peeling, flakes of green paint lie on the parquet, which is strewn with dust balls. Michał is staring out of the window, he'd like to see the bird feeding its young again, but the jay hasn't been back for some time. The policeman stands up and places a hand on his shoulder.

"Have you ever seen a dead person, one who's already far, far away in the sky? They can have their eyes open too."

"My granny, in a coffin, but not in the sky. Her cheeks were hanging down at the sides and her fingernails were even more purple."

"Purple?"

"Yeah, like methylated spirit that you have to mix with water, that kind of purple."

"And what were Bielecka's nails like?"

"I didn't see."

"So, what do you remember most? If you were going to remember one thing, what would it be?"

"Some little stones fell on her."

"How come?"

"I moved my leg and they fell down on her head. I didn't mean to, really, I just took a step and it happened."

"And then nothing, after the stones fell on her? She didn't move?"

"Nothing."

Michał stares out of the window again. The jay hasn't returned to its young, the nest is swaying in the wind. Maybe it's not for their mother that the chicks are screeching so loudly, but for fear that a tomcat will come, he thinks. He hears voices in the corridor, but the door doesn't open. Someone whispers something, then silence falls. The boy stops listening.

"She must have been dead already, then. And that's when Szary's daughter showed up, and your little pal Jodłowski?"

"They got there just after me."

"Did they say anything?"

"Weronika started crying, and Kuba said nothing. Sometimes that happens in dreams, you want to say something, but you try and nothing comes out. Kuba was like that until the next day, that's what my mum said."

"And you? What did you think?"

"That she'd always been sad."

"Who?"

"Pani Bielecka."

"And when would you have noticed something like that?"

"At the bakery, where else? She almost never smiled. I only saw her laugh once. She was standing in front of the bookshop, looking at the shelves and laughing."

"What a story! She was probably laughing at you, stuttering

and stammering. And what were you planning to nick from that hut?" asks the policeman suddenly.

"Nothing! I swear! There was no one there, but everything was neat and tidy, except the plates weren't washed, they still had red stains, from beetroot or something."

"Okay, okay, that'll do." The chief cuts him off. "Write that the hut was abandoned," he says, turning to the younger policeman. "And you didn't pass anyone at all on your way to the cliff?"

"Only one car went past when we were standing on the bridge."

"But no one saw it, not the girl, not your little pal, not you. You're all in agreement that you heard the water, not the car. Correct?"

"Dunno. I think we heard the car."

"I don't care what you think, just what you know. Write that the rush of the water made it impossible to clearly recognise other sounds," he dictates to the policeman. "And anyway, it's probably all down to the sadness, like the kid said," he adds more quietly.

When it's summer and the sun emits this strange yellow glow, sometimes I remember Małgorzata and my accident; as I said before, the two things go hand in hand. That she's there and I'm here. I used to see her every day, I didn't say that before, from the window of my watchmaker's shop. She'd run across the road with her bicycle as if she were running towards me, the pavement was very narrow there, only one person could fit, but there were never any accidents. She was so close that I could observe her carefully, I'd always liked her, since we were little, we were in the same class but I never told her, that's just how life goes. She waved hello to me every day, but other than that we didn't communicate. Did people talk about her around here? No, as if she were invisible, and yet she served people bread every day with her lovely, well-groomed hands. It was only after her death that they began to remember she'd left her fiancé just before the wedding, and that perhaps over the years she had been overwhelmed with despair, but to hold sorrow in your heart for that long and then go and throw yourself off a cliff? People didn't think it was possible. Others said that she was punished by God because you can't treat a man that way if he professes his love and buys a ring. Unless, as some people said, she was mad, because she barely spoke, so no one could get to know her. Or that it was because of the high heels – her foot slipped and she went flying, bit the dust, and if only she'd been wearing flats, then maybe she would have regained her balance at the last minute. And people stopped venturing out there for a good couple of years, some were a bit scared that maybe someone had helped her in her descent, I don't know, who am I to judge. Has anything changed here? Nothing at all, the people are still the same, there are just some new shops, the tenements have been renovated, and the station building now houses a small railway museum. Everyone still goes to the Ropa river to swim, where else? Some, like me, seek out the greatest depths, others just go in up to their knees and they're done. She had no close relatives, nobody. Some distant cousins took on her house, meaning they come for the holidays; the rest of the year everything's locked and bolted. They pay locals to mow the lawn, prune the trees in the orchard, and in the winter – when everything freezes over – someone goes to turn off the water.

White Nights

It was getting dark by four o'clock, not everyone can cope with that. The frozen snow crunches underfoot and you look behind you every now and then, if you dare. And if not, you just speed up to lose whoever's following you. Imagine, for the first few weeks you go out after dark and you keep stumbling – here, a long-buried stone jutting out; there, the fallen branch that's not yet rotted; or, most annoying of all, some tourist has crushed a can and thrown it in the middle of the road, and when there's a ground frost, you can really go flying on a can like that. At first, you grope your way around, even when the stars are shining, they don't give off any brightness. Same with the snow. In theory, you know everything's covered in white, but the eye has to adjust. It's black all around and you're just trying to make out your neighbours' house near the forest – are they already asleep, not asleep, getting ready for bed, or maybe they're fucking, who was in the mood first today? You want to go in and ask: "Can I take your wife? We could switch for a while. You come to my place, I'll have it warm and cosy for you, you'll stay for two weeks, and we'll take it from there." Various things come to mind when you're standing there and you know that life's going on nearby, but you settle down when you remember that you came here not to live, but to die.

At first, even when you've got the hang of the route a little, you don't go far and you always leave the light on in the entrance hall, winter or summer. That's why, I reckon, it's good to have a dog with you, although if it suddenly stops, raises its head, and stares at one spot, you'd better not think too hard about what's out there glowering at you. Cos a dog will sniff out both a spirit and a wild animal, although these days I know that neither will come close, each one is as shy as the other. But every day you grow bolder, the darkness gets less and less dark, you go a few feet further, the rotten branch, even if it's still hanging, doesn't bother you anymore, nor the stone. Then, as long as there's lots of stars in the sky, you start to see shapes – in the summer, hay bales, the self-built tractors left out for the next day, rakes leaning against bushes, scythes hung on cherry tree branches. Later, you know from memory that you're standing by the dried-up apple tree, which, no matter if it's November or June, always hangs on to a few leaves. Before you know it, you reach the last house, where the pale light of the TV flashes into the darkness, and when you gaze at it for a moment, you feel like you haven't woken up yet. And if you went inside, all your dead would be sitting on the chairs and beds. Backs straight, hands in their laps, they'd be staring at the blank, flickering screen, the light drawing them in. And if you were standing nearby, they'd look at you with bared teeth, as if on cue, but there's no going back, the door's closed. This is the dream I sometimes have at night and I don't want to wake up from it.

But before I came here, my dreams were no different.

"Andrzej, Andrzej, get up! Mum'll get angry that nothing's done and she'll whinge about me," Henia pleads. "You can see my belly's in the way so I can't bend down."

"Alright, I'll get up in a minute," he replies and covers his head with the blanket.

Today I'll tell her I'm going, thinks Andrzej. She can do what she wants, they can't keep me here forever. It's over.

"Why are you just lying there? It's so cold today! Mum went to the neighbours', been gone an hour, they're probably talking shit about everyone. I gotta tell you, the baby was kicking all night! I couldn't get to sleep, I was tossing and turning, closing my eyes, opening them, but it didn't help. After me, you're gonna be the first person in the world this little one sees," says Henia, suddenly speaking softly, placing her brother's hand on her stomach. "You won't feel nothing now, it was busy all night, it needs to get some sleep," she says with a cheerful laugh.

"Heńka, I'm leaving in two days," says Andrzej, not taking his hand off his sister's stomach.

For a moment, Henia looks once again like the little girl who, when placed in front of a large map, couldn't locate the capital of Poland, so just looked down at her feet and drilled a hole in the floor with the pointer, as if wanting to dig a tunnel and escape.

"But there ain't no market in two days, so where'd you be going, and what for?" she asks quietly.

"Yeah, I'm not going to market. But it's not far, less than twenty miles from here, hardly the other side of the world. To be fair, there's no bus, but Pilot got a job there too, and

Piotrek, so we'll come over in the Maluch from time to time. I'm off to the trees, there's not much to do here, and there's so much forest over there, more than a lifetime's worth."

"So Piotrek's off the idea of slaughtering pigs?"

"He'll never go off it, but he's got a girl there, says he wants to get married, then he probably won't come back here. And Pilot, we'll see if he keeps his job. Maybe he'll just fire up a plane and fly here," Andrzej says, trying to make his sister laugh.

"I'd come with you in a flash, I'll pack up my togs, I won't say a word on the way, I'll cook, clean, wash your socks…?"

"It's a single room, Heńka, holes in the windows and doors so big you have to plug them with rags. And what about the baby?"

"Maybe you've met a girl there too, you just won't admit it!"

"Give it a rest, Heńka! I'm going to work, there's no room for birds with kids."

"So maybe you'll meet someone. Clearly, if Piotrek's dragging you God knows where like a dog sniffing out bitches. And more important," she says, welling up, "ain't you going to hold the baby for the christening?"

"We'll see, four more months, who knows what'll happen?"

"And what if I don't want you no more? Maybe I'll find someone else who won't turn on us like Judas," adds Henia tearfully.

"Heńka, the real father can hold the baby, just leave me alone, I don't have to explain myself to you."

"But you said we were forever, that even if a fire or a flood came, you'd take me on your back and hold me up high, so no water or fire would touch me. How many days have you known you're running away from us?"

"I'm not running away, I'm going to work! Three weeks ago Piotrek told me, and I agreed, I didn't think twice. And I told you all that stuff cos we were little then. Heńka, it's time to grow up, what will you tell your kid?"

"Probably just that promises come cheap. Here I am, walking round by your side all these months, letting you put your hands on my belly, and now they're around my neck? And who's going to save you there, next time you're at death's door? That last time, when you were foaming at the mouth…"

Andrzej gets close to her, raises his hand, but lets it fall again.

"Don't you worry, I'm sure some bitch will take care of this dog. You're better off keeping an eye out for death, if not for life."

I don't remember much about those last two days at home. I think that's how it goes, when an image stabs you in the heart, you tell your mind to forget it. At least that's how it was for me. I didn't have much to pack, socks, pants, a couple of jumpers and shirts, three pairs of trousers, a heavy jacket, and a brand-new chainsaw, which I'd bought in secret before I knew about the job. The forestry ones didn't slice into the wood so smoothly, they started shuddering and you had to keep tightening the chain. I'd hidden the new one in the attic, but it wasn't long before it was put to use. It was beautiful, orange, heavy enough, and it fit the hands perfectly. I often went up to the attic to look at it; I'd unwrap it from the rag, wipe it off, and then one day Piotrek stopped me at Kazek's shop and asked if I wanted to go away to work.

"It's less than twenty miles to Kunkowa, but be prepared, it's worse than here, you'll want to scarper after a month or two. And nothing to fuck, unless you fuck each other. Cos I won't let you near my girl, I'm telling you, she's the most gorgeous, anyway, you'll see for yourself. You and Pilot would work in the forest, and I'd be the new butcher there, apparently the old one makes watery black pudding with lint inside, people throw it to the dogs, they're all so fussy. So? Sound good, or are you staying here cooped up with your mummy and little sis?"

I must have spoken to Henia about something during that time, but I don't remember a single word, though I can recall that conversation with Piotrek in detail, even when he winked, and what the weather was like. The sun was shining brightly, small flakes of snow settled on his hair and his quilted jacket, for a moment I even thought that he looked like a six-year-old boy again, his cheeks red from the cold, that any moment we'd take our sledges, sneak a cigarette each from our fathers and go plummeting downhill from the upper road. And we'd only return home in the late afternoon, when our mothers started calling us and bleating on that it was dark. We'd be soaked all the way to our pants and we'd get belted on the back, but gently this time, cos it was a small offence, and we'd fall asleep feverish, not because we were ill, but because we were happy.

"I'm going," I said.

Did Henia say goodbye to me? All I remember is looking out of the Maluch's rear window, and she was standing to the side and looking at the road along which we were about to disappear. She had her hands on her hips, as she always did when she was staring at something, as if it would keep her upright for longer. The sun was reflecting off the snow, I could barely see her, and by the time we reached the turn-off to Rożnowice, she resembled a small black mark on a white background. I held my bag of clothes in my lap and squeezed my eyes shut as tight as I could.

We were there in under an hour.

It was a long road down into the village, forest on both sides, the weather was bad, snow and rain were pounding the car windows, but Piotrek kept his foot on the accelerator.

"If you were about to get laid, you'd be flooring it too," he said, whooping with laughter and nudging my shoulder.

At the very bottom of the hill there was an Orthodox church and a cemetery, a few houses along the road, nothing more, a small, fast-flowing river, wide in some places, must have been lovely to swim there in the summer. The people sat in their houses, a few dogs reluctantly stuck their muzzles out of their kennels. The village was like a ghost town wiped out by leprosy or cholera that hadn't been discovered yet. I imagined whole families sitting withered at their tables, set with plates and cutlery, a soup tureen uncovered, but only dust and dead flies at the bottom. Or they were sleeping in their beds, or someone else's bed, when death caught them. And we sped in the orange Maluch through this emptiness, where the snow was slowly giving way to mud and frozen meadows.

"Right, lads, out you get. I'm going on to Usta, I wouldn't last a second in this shithole. Just right for you," he chuckled. "Now piss off!"

Pilot was sitting in the back, just finishing his fourth beer. He got out of the car, shaky and taciturn.

"I was always meant to be here," I told him.

A hut is a hut. I didn't need any luxuries. Fifteen guys, almost all our age, most of them with wives and children waiting at home, others corroded by moonshine distilled at night and the most disgusting cigs from God knows where. Up at dawn, quick march into the woods when it's nearby, or a lift when it's further away, work, silence punctuated by the shrill whistling of saws and the hammering of wedges, and to help pass the time: cigarettes, a hip flask pulled out every now and then and the same jokes told on repeat. It was only that orange chainsaw that kept me alive. I've always feared silence, I felt that if it was silent, you'd die, or lose your hearing and voice forever. When I was a child, I used to go with Piotrek and Pilot to the scrubland and, so that it wouldn't be quiet, I would hit the trees with sticks. I remember that sound – it seemed short, but it was strong enough to rip through the silence, rending it, creating an echo. Push, release, push, release, that's how I work now, nose to the grindstone. Not all trees yield right away, some need to be pruned properly before they fall. Those are the ones with the strongest will to live, but once you've started, you can't leave them mutilated. It's the same with animals, when you see one that's sick, or hit by a car, you have to finish it off, find a stone, a brick, or a shoe, if you're brave enough. The worst thing is when a tree starts to creak just before it falls, that means it's begging for mercy, and then I have to cover my ears for a minute, although I'm scared that I might not return to the living.

Henia gave birth to a girl.

No, I didn't go to the christening. Pilot was sacked almost immediately; he lasted maybe a month, he hadn't been showing up for shifts or was so drunk that two of us couldn't hold him upright. So I had no one to chat to, and I saw the others sniggering at me, the fact that I didn't take breaks, that I didn't know any jokes. Piotrek practically stopped driving over our way, he didn't really have a reason to come, he put tinted side windows in the Maluch, he slaughtered one pig after another, they said he knew his stuff.

"When I've got blood on my hands and face, that's when I'm happiest," he told me. "Seriously, no woman is as warm inside as the belly of an animal that's just been cut open. Try it sometime, if your love life ever dries up."

Piotrek and Pilot. We'd always stuck together since we were little, nothing connects people like welts on your backs and arses, though I actually got the shit beaten out of me the least. Of the three of us, Pilot had it the worst, both his parents thrashed him equally, sometimes he didn't even want to sit down cos his arse hurt so much. And he was born with those freakish eyes, each going in a different direction, he always looked upwards, at the sky, cos he could see the best that way, that's why we called him Pilot. Sometimes I thought they were beating him not for any particular wrongdoing, but because he was born so ugly. And just as everyone expected, he was the first of us to pop his clogs, though I thought it would be me, cos we were always racing in that department – he in his way, I in mine. No, I didn't go to the funeral, Piotrek weaselled out of it, and I didn't dare ask anyone else to go with me. I don't blame him at all, it was obvious he was stuck fast to his girl, he clearly had no desire to loosen the stitches, cos once they're undone, it's hard to sew them back together as strong. I'm not gonna lie, when that day and hour came, I felt like someone had put a sack over my head and was tightening it with all their might. What had they dressed him in? Did they at least buy new shoes, or did they send him off in the ones that were falling to pieces? Did they fasten his shirt all the way up to the neck, or sloppily, every other button? And did they close his eyes, or leave them so that he'd be a laughingstock in

the next world as well? At twelve o'clock I put down my saw
and looked at the ground like you'd look at a freshly dug grave.

Piotrek came to see me a few days after the funeral, but he
wasn't alone.

She got out of the car. In a red dress with black polka
dots, narrow at the waist and wide from the hips; over that
she wore a fitted jacket, and her shiny brown hair fell below
her shoulders. Not too tall, round breasts – just right, like
my saw, for holding in your hands. Swaying hips, strong legs,
small mouth, but the most beautiful eyes: deep blue, like the
sky when snow's about to fall.

"This is Anka, my fiancée. She's going to milk the cows
here. She's a hairdresser, but the salon's closed down, so until something comes up, she'll stay here to earn some money,
she'll sleep at the farmer's place. And I'm off to Germany for
two months to slaughter their pigs. We're building a house,
didn't I tell you? We need the cash, so even hands like hers
have to get to work," Piotrek said with a laugh. "Go on, Anka,
the farmer's cottage is down there, I'm right behind you, go
and say hello and get changed," he said, and the girl left without a word.

What's the timbre of her voice? I wondered. Does she
speak high or low, soft or loud, or maybe she stutters, doesn't
pronounce her "r"s, or sounds as clear and pure as a famous
singer? How would she say my name if I stopped her now,
grabbed her by the arms, knocked her over and pinned her to
the ground? Or would she still not speak, just stare at me with
those deep blue eyes?

"Listen," Piotrek said, lowering his voice and coming closer, "keep an eye on her here, I mean not on her, but on the

lads, cos she's not like that, although these people will probably say all sorts of things. If you notice one of them taking longer breaks, for example, or hanging around the farmer's cottage, you'll tell me straight away. You can shag her once, it's different with you, we grew up together, you're practically my brother," he said seriously. "Maybe you fancy it now? I'll be happy to watch, she likes it best standing up. Unless you don't feel like it now, then you know for the future. I always said you have to keep an eye out for your own, didn't I?"

The orange Maluch had disappeared over the horizon, but the music from the radio on full blast still carried over the fields.

Anna, as she liked to be called, had a voice that was low and quiet. She didn't talk to me much, sometimes just about the house, that they would have two floors, each with a bathroom, they would put a large bed and a TV in the bedroom, definitely tiles in the kitchen, and the outside would be painted willow or peach, they didn't know yet. That Piotrek would drive down and then back again every now and then, and she would go back to her trade and cut hair, cos that's what she did best.

"Cows aren't for me," she would say, putting the ends of her hair in her mouth, or rubbing her hips or shoulders as if she were cold.

I never kissed her, but a couple of times I looked into her eyes and felt that I'd seen them before: they were empty, unmoving, and they looked like the eyes of my grandmother Stefania, whom I'd found dead on the floor.

"Her heart stopped," said the doctor, but I think it didn't stop, it just froze over.

No, I wasn't going to tell on Anna, although I knew one of the young sawyer's assistants was sneaking out to see her at night, and he had a wife and four children, and was so poor that he'd come away to work in a thin jacket with holes in it.

Anyway, I didn't have to bring it up. Piotrek didn't return from abroad. No, he had no way of knowing what was going on here, that's just how it turned out, no one forced him to stay. They say he met a rich widow and opened a sausage shop. Now he's speeding on German roads, and the music from the radio on full blast carries like bad news.

All I know about Anna is that the forest guy also ran out on her.

I thought I'd wait until late autumn. When things were slow, and the wind was blowing, I'd watch for hours as it swept through the grasses and changed their colour, and at night I'd walk in the dark, I knew it by heart and eventually the dogs even stopped barking at me.

"Misiek, Nero, Pepper!" I'd call to them by name and they'd wag their tails or not even come out of their kennels.

And then it was a late afternoon in September, a Friday, I remember that clearly.

"Are you going with us to the dance?" one of the lads asked, cos he knew I'd probably say no.

"I'm going," I replied.

We packed ourselves into four cars, it was all the lads had been thinking about for weeks. Dressed up, but the dirt beneath our fingernails was black. It gets deep inside you and then you can scrub all your life but it won't come out. I didn't turn around once, afraid I'd see Pilot or Anna calling me back. We parked outside the hospital.

"I'll just get some cigarettes, I'll be right back." I remember that's all I told them, and I ran as fast as I could towards the marketplace in Zawodzie, then across the bridge to the square, past the tax office, to the bus station. The driver was finishing off his cigarette, I knew him by sight, everyone knows everyone round here.

"We'll crank the destination sign over to Rzepiennik in a moment," he said, and flicked his cigarette butt into the air. "Look, the embers separated from the fag-end, that was pretty, eh? And what are you up to? Finished your shift?"

I just nodded.

Henia was standing outside the house with her hands on her hips. She stretched her dress down to hide her big post-pregnancy belly.

"You're here," she said. Nothing else.

Maria

Every evening, when I close the gates, when I gather up the scattered hoes and rakes and put them away in the cupboard, come cold or rain or wind or fug, I stop at the threshold and watch as darkness dissolves all the shapes. I look longest at the oak tree, which once was struck by lightning and sprouted a miniature tree on one of its branches. And if someone asked me why I was standing like that, I'd say: I don't dream anymore, but I still hear the music.

> Little rue, grow tall and wise,
> Oh, how very deep he lies.
> How the rue has grown ahead,
> Hark, the lady never wed.
> Peer into the dark woods, lass,
> See who's on their way to us.
> Men are coming, broken-hearted,
> Brothers of the man departed.

On the day of the wedding, I stood in the doorway, as I am now, and looked at the weather-beaten face of my father, who was wiping his nose on a grey handkerchief; at the restless eyes of Zofia, who was gawping at the ground and talking quietly to herself; I looked for Hanna and it was only after a while that I noticed she had turned her back on everyone and was staring at the reaped fields. I could never guess what she was thinking about. None of us could, not Father or Zofia either. From a young age she'd been secretive, she hid everything inside, even when she burst out laughing, it was like she was going inwards, maybe someone else lived within her and only they knew her secrets? But she was always the first to give commands. As a child, she used to boss me and Zofia around, and since she was the oldest and the prettiest, she was allowed to do everything. Later on, she pretended not to remember telling us to jump into the well. First we'd listened closely, because she'd said that Mother was calling us from there. Mother had been dead for a year, and Hanna said that we had to go down and fetch her. Zofia was tiny, maybe five years old. We listened, our ears pressed to the well, and we even thought we could hear her saying, "My little ones, come and get me, it's cold and lonely here." But everyone hears what they want to hear. When we brought this up with Hanna later on, she didn't own up to it.

"Where did you read that fairy tale?" she asked us, although neither of us were into books.

Hanna had finished school, she was meant to stay in the city, marry the best bachelors, but she came back, I don't know what for, other than to go to waste.

Three months before my wedding, and I resented her for a long time for this, she had walked into the river up to her neck with heavy stones in her pockets. Probably there

wouldn't have been a wedding if she'd succeeded, at the time
that seemed like the end of the world, today I see things differently. Everyone knew straight away that Zofia wasn't all
there, but no one could figure out what was up with Hanna.
The men flocked to her, they wanted to marry her, but she
knew what she was doing, she waved everyone away. And
sometimes I wished that someone would wave her away too,
so maybe my wish had come true? Sometimes I liked the guys
who were stalking Hanna, but I never said a word, and sometimes I even went to the kitchen, behind the house or into
the orchard, just to cry. All I heard was her giggling with a
mousey squeal or saying something I didn't understand. So
she went, it was thirty years ago now, to the river... But that
day it was me, not her, standing in a white dress and listening
to the music:

> Girl, why do you stand 'neath the sycamore tree?
> Does the sun burn your face, are
> they rain clouds you see?
> I don't fear the sun, I'm not scared of the rain,
> I'm just waiting for Janek, who's late home again.
> Jump, jump now, tralalalala – Jump, jump now, hey!

The music played louder and louder, and Antek, hunched
over, was walking towards me. The first time I saw him, he'd
been walking just as slowly towards me. He's in no rush, I'd
thought, so perhaps he'll go through life just the same, little
by little, and he'll evade evil. But now they were picking me
up and carrying me to him, I felt as if I could catch a cloud
and warm my hands on the sun. They took us to the dance,
spun us around, and I watched Antek disappear and reappear.

Two days after the wedding, Antek came on his wagon

to pick me up, I already had everything packed. There wasn't much: sheets, four plates, five cups, three pots, two nightgowns, some clothes and underwear. There were still a few pounds of meat left from the wedding, so I divided it equally between us and my family. I didn't take the moonshine, let Father have it if he needs it. I was standing in front of the house and I saw Antek waving at me from afar, so I raised both hands like someone who's suddenly decided to surrender. Zofia cuddled up to me and cried, asking me not to go, Hanna didn't look me in the eye, even for a second. Father stood as still as he had at Mother's funeral. It was hot, Antek was panting and sweating, he picked me up and sat me on the wagon.

"Don't look back at them," he said.

So I didn't see the dust slowly covering them. All I heard was the dog's barking, which accompanied us all the way to the Swedish Deluge burial mound. There everything fell silent. Did my father wave to me? Had Zofia stopped crying? What was Hanna staring at? I sat upright and I didn't say a word cos I was afraid of what sound might emerge from my throat. It's no easier saying goodbye to those who are alive than to those who are already in the grave. You have to wonder if they've put rags in the windows for winter, or what they see when they close their eyes just before falling asleep, I thought.

Off I rode, as if I was never coming back.

Darkness was falling slowly. I snuggled into Antek's shoulder and felt the warmth of his body. People were coming down from the fields, calling to their children and dogs to start heading inside, the day was coming to an end. My mother used to call to us the same way when my sisters and I were building dens in the scrubland: she'd stand in front of the house and shout our names. All the mothers in Binarowa used to call to their children like that in the evenings, cos they knew that night changes the shape of all things and when something approaches the house in the dark, you never know if it might not be in human form. A mother's voice was like a predetermined signal that it was time to shake off leaves and dirt, drop your sticks, and run as fast as you could. The chill of the approaching night engulfed warm bodies, and it became so quiet that the only sound was the patter of small feet on the ground. Children ran down from the forests, hills and fields, happy and horrified to have once again escaped the darkness, which for a brief time forced them to squint when they came into the light.

"We have so much time ahead of us," said Antek suddenly. But he had that cloudy water in his eyes that seeped in when sorrow gripped his heart.

For some the voice trembles, for others it shows in the eyes, I thought.

See the girl watching, fitfully she waits.
Yearning for Janek, how her heart aches.
But Janek went to war, Janek was killed,
Now he's lying in a bloody field.
Jump, jump now, tralalalala – Jump, jump now, hey!

Now that summer's coming, I have to wait longer for it to get dark. I hear the cries of mothers, fainter, and the running of children, racing against something that will catch them anyway. If only you knew that the thing behind your back, from which you're fleeing, striding with your short, strong legs, doesn't stay at the gate, behind the door, but comes into the brightness with you, stuck like an invisible skin. And even if you soon readjust to the light, a small dark blotch will gather in the corners of your eyes, and one day it will flood your vision. For Antek, that blotch was growing month on month.

"I'm off towards Przemyśl, I'll be back in a year or two, I can't stay here any longer," he said at last.

It was late October, the light was different, it gave off a sudden yellow glow, only to fade quickly. I was standing there in my thicker dress, holding a bucket of milk. I let go of the wire handle with the smooth wooden grip. Creamy, white milk soaks into the earth almost as quickly as water, I thought to myself. The next day he was already packed. I threw myself down on my knees so he wouldn't go, but he just walked around me. I stared after him until he became a small, almost invisible dot and disappeared. I never found out why he left, nor have I ever heard of anyone else here leaving everything overnight, taking almost nothing with them and disappearing. I'd go outside every evening and call his name, and his name mingled with all the children's names that the mothers yelled. And when Antek left, that's when I stopped dreaming – my eyes were open even in my sleep, cos if he came, I wanted to see him straight away.

At first, I told people he was away working, but after a while everyone stopped believing me. My strength diminished with each passing month, the cows went without water, the horse was hungry, the hens were covered in shit. I couldn't even hold my arms in the air for more than a few seconds, but the worst was yet to come. I sold everything including the field for next to nothing, I just kept the house, and then they started coming in, sitting on my bed, talking to me. They came one after the other. In the small hours, when my eyes were still crusty with sleep, I heard their whistling right beside my ear, as if they couldn't speak in human language as the good Lord commanded. But He must have commanded again, cos when they came in the daytime, they would mumble. They said the houses there were well-kept, there were more than enough potatoes, that the cows gave the purest milk and their udders never bled. But apparently, that summer they had all gone hopping mad, and the pus and blood had to be squeezed out first so that the children wouldn't go hungry.

"Anyone who says they're disgusted has never felt hunger, because hunger doesn't start in the belly. First it enters the head and goes straight to the heart," they said and pointed at each other's heads, then they beat their chests.

But they recounted that sometimes people would shit themselves from hunger, although it should be the other way around, when the stomach's empty but a draught blows through it like a house with broken windows. But they'd shit themselves, and the basins had to be taken out, and the sheets washed, even though they were dripping like after a big storm. When the sun was shining and a warm wind was blowing, everything would dry in a flash, but when the damp came, it had to be dried inside the house and no one was disgusted then either, nor did they say that those who were shitting should be moved to the barn. They all slept like brothers and sisters, and even dreamed the same dreams, for the hearts of the hungry are alike. And their dreams were not of a hog with chestnuts for eyes and a red apple in its mouth, nor of heavy cream running down their chins and chests. They dreamed that they were standing in a wardrobe, in pairs, covering the mouths of babies so that no one would hear them cry. They told me things like that.

And they'd call to me at night: "Take the shovel, you'll find it in the shed. No, not the one that couldn't even fell a chicken. The one leaning there behind the quern stones. You could kill a goat with that. There's a body, so take the shovel and hurry, you have to dig before it cools down."

And I'd walk with the shovel, and they'd shout, harrying me, baring their rotten teeth and drooling. With my shovel, I'd walk straight, as if to a wedding, holding the hem of my skirt in one hand, I practised my steps, I bowed. They were calling me, so I went to them, I had no one else. The ground was opening up, soil was falling on my head, in my mind they just kept muttering: "The earth is hard, you have to roll up your skirt, take off your knickers and give the earth what it's due."

"And what would you give hard, dry earth?" I'd ask.

"A girl's little fingers, a girl's little feet, a girl's little eyes. And she whimpered and cried, until she was burnt and fried. Her mouth was calling and calling, and then we brought hay, hey-hey. And the ground is so fucking hard, we shan't dig," they'd reply.

So I'd start taking the shovel back, but they'd shout louder and louder.

"I'll set my hair on fire," I threatened them, "I'll gouge out my eyes, maybe you'll go back where you belong. And I won't dream anymore, nothing will come to me ever again," I shouted, and prayed for death.

At the end of winter, on the same wagon on which I'd arrived at Antek's, they took me back to Hanna, Zofia and my father. The neighbours had found me curled up in front of the shed. It's a good thing it had already thawed, or I'd have frozen solid. The dreams never came back, the dead spoke to me less and less, I just saw them in the distance sometimes, and then everything stopped. I never heard anything about Antek. No one here remembers him anymore, only I can attest to his existence.

You heard the music, dear Hanna, you loved it so,
When they played like sweet night-
ingales 'neath the window.
Your pinafore silver, from Mother, we're told,
A fine string of beads and a bodice embroidered in gold.
Today you are like a white rose in a garden so green,
Tomorrow you'll be like a lily, serene
on the water, a lily serene.

And now I stand here in the doorway every night when Hanna and Zofia are asleep. I look at things, plants and birds that disappear as soon as night falls on them. At first, I see everything in a haze, then nothing at all. But with time, my eyes adjust to the darkness and I can make out what's lying in front of the smokehouse and what's under the tree, what kind of moth is circling above me and trying to land in my hair. The burnt oak, which sprouted a miniature tree on its branch, is still racing upwards, still trying to draw the last goodness from the soil, and I'm waiting for the day when it has sucked up all it can and falls down so quietly that even the most vigilant dog won't hear it. Only that music starts up when I stand here. First, the violin plays a tune so mournful it almost brings tears to your eyes, but then the accordion comes in and drowns out the sorrow.

Anielka

It's cold because it keeps raining and raining. For days we've been thinking about what to hunt for dinner, what little creature to cook up from Grandad's recipe. He was a good man, that's what Pani Owczarowa says. He chased after the Germans with pitchforks, and then they drank vodka together. As a smoke screen. Behind the smoke screen, he put on a heavy sheepskin coat and went off to search for little ginger heads, little bowlegs, and sacks stuffed with money. Like that aunt who buried a jar of gold in the garden, and now she's toe-tapping in her coffin. Under the fence, where the large currants grow, she hid five rings, three silver-plated rosaries, three communion rosaries, one signet ring and a gemstone – a sapphire, supposedly, because it shone deep blue. The bells chime, it's almost midday. Remember when Whiskers was struggling for breath in the cesspit? He waved his little paws about till his eyes watered. And that other cat that got scalded with tar? They say it was thrown in the vat in an act of revenge. Neighbour is wolf to neighbour – a wolf with a red, bushy tail.

It's almost midday. Grandad walks on with a bundle of straw and matches that the rain won't wet through, because they're well-made and German. Grandad is staggering from the wind and the rowanberry vodka he found in the barn, where no people were burnt, only little ginger heads. Ahoy, captain! Tenth of December, it's time to catch the kids! He walks on, because he's not afraid of the cold. He has thick boots stuffed with newspaper, and a sheepskin hat. (Teddy, Teddy, aren't you missing the sun, the green grass?). Teddy was little when Grandma found him by the brook. Hop, little lamb in the bag and straight to the pen. (Teddy, Teddy, grow big and round!) She'd picked the alfalfa from fields belonging to their neighbours – the ones who hadn't been killed, who'd just gone on a trip; everything had been empty there for a long time. She drew well water, because it was uncontaminated – evil is immune to evil, so it's okay to drink from those springs. And grow, grow up to the sky. Grandad walks on. Grandma rolls up her sleeves at home. Crackling and onions sizzle on the stove. Grandad is lashed by the wind, so he fastens his sheepskin coat. Grandma is lashed by the heat, so she untucks her blouse. Jan – Grandad, the untiring carpenter – doesn't know that as soon as he gives up the ghost in an orchard full of blossoming apple trees, Grandma will board a train to the Baltic Sea to take a photo with Franz. Snap, hand on the shoulder. Snap, hand on the knee. Tralalala-hey-hey-hey, now there'll be no further pain. Tralalala-yo-ho-ho, flies are buzzing to and fro. Squash the housefly on your knee. Squash the housefly, one two three. They always hung flypaper. The flies would twitch on the paper, shaking their abdomens. It's a long death. The death of martyrs and heroes.

"That's how heroes die, without a peep," Grandad Jan said.

The ones that fell in the line of Grandad's fire also died without a word. While the village was languishing under the bedsheets, Grandad used to put on his sheepskin coat, take a box of matches, crumple up some newspapers and out he'd go.

New wood panelling inside the house. Not like those blackened planks that Grandma said were lying around at the redheads' farm. New, spotless. Like they have at the house of Pan Władek, the militiaman, who now makes everyone call him a policeman. No traces of greasy little paws, no flies, no saliva. If you run your hand over it, you'll smell pine and glue. We will celebrate the panelling for a long time, invite the neighbours, put out vodka with the cheapest orange squash, which smells like unaired bedding. For a while, the animals will find a place in our home. Here, Whiskers, drink some milk. Here, Teddy, eat some hay. Here's a bed for the pig, here's a space for the horse. We will take down the fly-paper for a week – no longer, because the panelling will get flyspecked again, and Mama will have to wipe it with a cloth every hour. So the flies will land on Mama's back, on Papa's leg, on Grandma's thigh and on Franz's hairy chest. We will cook sour rye soup in the largest pot and stomp on cabbage in the barrel where we once stored a pig for a rainy day. Franz will not stomp on the cabbage, because the salt shrinks his feet and other parts that Grandma only talks about quietly at confession. So I, Anielka, will hop into the barrel. I'm three foot seven and weigh as much as an imported lamb. I know because Daddy put me on the poultry seller's scales once. What a tiny girl, no more than a few hens! So I will hop in and I'll stomp all day long. And until the first juices come out, I will dance like I'm in a meadow. Jump-hey-hey-hey, jump-hey-ho, Papa and I to the woods we'll go. In the woods are boars and deer, if you shout they'll disappear. Me and you are rubber and glue, you're the one who stinks of poo. I'll stomp until the mosquitoes swarm, until the owls fall silent, until the sparrows chirp: it's done.

"More salt," my mother will say, "because it's not releasing juice."

And I'll stomp until the field poppies get redder, until Mongrel tucks his tail between his legs and eats all the fleas. Until my mother's wrinkles slacken like my other grandma's when she was dying.

New panelling and Papa in a ditch. It shines because Mama runs a rag over it every day and says: "This panelling will outlive everyone, because it's new, not like those planks left lying around after the redheads were gone. Those people stank everything up and went off on a trip to catch fish while sitting on the riverbed."

Papa in a ditch. The sun's shining, sultry and oppressive, it'll be a sticky kind of day. Kasia's already walking along the edge of the meadow, Tomek's emerging from the forest and soon they will see that Papa's in the ditch and he isn't coming. Kasia has ladybirds pinned in her hair, they don't speck the walls like our flies. Catch a housefly in a jar, make a few holes and it'll turn my fair hair golden. It sparkles like a star in the sky, Grandad sending a message from far away. He shines a light so that I, Anielka, can find my way to Papa, who isn't getting up. Kasia runs with her red backpack, uncle brought her wax crayons, she draws butterflies with multi-coloured heads. The butterflies fly around the meadow and pollinate the world into more colours than they have themselves. Here my little brother's hair is purple, there our uncle's moustache is orange. Mummy has polka dot knickers and Daddy has rust-coloured socks. Papa has no socks, so he won't come. Go get Papa's socks, find the ones he wears on Sundays, it'll get him up quicker. And he has no shoes. Go get Papa's shoes, bring the ones he wears for name days, he'll think it's a celebration and he'll get up. And Kasia's just coming. Nearly here, you can see her white tights, washed yesterday, because Kasia's things get washed every day. Not once a fortnight, but always when she gets home from school. Her hair also gets washed three times a week, not just on Saturday when the hens have been slaughtered and all the feathers are dry. Kasia smells like suncream because she has sensitive skin. Kasia does not smell like laundry soap or the nettle shampoo that makes white flakes fall from the scalp. The huge snowdrifts would cover the whole farmyard and Papa in the ditch.

They did the new panelling for Mateuszek's communion. My little brother, who is two heads taller than me and weighs not as much as an imported lamb, but as much as our sow Lusia, who is now a sausage ring on the communion table. She graces that table, she shimmers, she sprawls, so majestic! But where is the place for the hen? And where is the place for Teddy? The sow always liked to be the centre of attention. She used to run out when Grandma was bringing in the pigswill. And sploosh, right in the gob. Lusia's lips were painted with Mama's pink lipstick to confuse people. Lusia did not want to hang upside down like Saint Andrew. Papa knows all the saints and he told me to pray to Saint Rita. Rita-tita, wouldn't wanna meet her. My little brother liked the new panelling. At night, he would carve numbers into it, the numbers that Grandad told him to memorise when he was still alive. I don't know if they were car registration numbers, house numbers, the number of chickens, or maybe the eggs laid by the guinea hens. But my little brother remembered, even though he had lice, which eat away at the memory. Just like they ate a piece of Kazio and Monisia's heads and minds. They lived down by the brook, my little brother and I used to go to their place in the school holidays. Mama said that when Kazio was little, he cried a lot because his bum was covered in a rash. He was as speckled as the ladybird in Kasia's hair. He'd scramble around and wave his arms about like a swimmer who'd crossed the seven seas. Kazio, Kazio, fly up high, bring us down a piece of pie. But he didn't fly off. He lay wrapped up like a mummy when the sun was baking, and bees would fly over him. And Monisia had brown freckles on her belly, on her legs, even in her ear.

"It's from hunger and cold," said Mama.

"What cold, Mama, the sun's always shining."

Granny said that when they'd escaped, she was the same age as me. Sharik the horse carried her, her mother, father and little brother Stefanek. There was nothing in the wagon, because Grandma's daddy's sheepskin coat was too thick and they couldn't fit anything else. Even the rabbit stayed behind in the shed. Don't worry, Ears, we'll be back tomorrow! Here's some water, here are some sweet apples, here's a drop of milk and a little clover. Tomorrow, or the day after at the latest, I'll bring you fresh apples from the orchard, some strawberries, a bit of honey, and a whole handful of dandelions. You'll eat and drink until you burst like the Wawel Dragon. A smooch on the nose, a smooch on the paw. Bye, see you tomorrow! Sharik raced onwards, and Granny's daddy was lashed by the wind. Giddy up, hey-ho, it's not off to school we go! Granny didn't go to school anymore after that. Wasps buzzed above her head as Sharik's mane blew in the easterly wind, which is always warmer because it blows from the ocean, where jellyfish bask in the sun and crabs walk sideways. The wasps were cross with Grandma because she'd tripped up her friend, the one who didn't want to get on the train. Granny, Granny, hey-hey-hey, will there be much pain today? Granny always ties my fair hair in a plait. I don't like plaits, because the horse in the stable also has a braided tail. What? Bay, who's a boy, disguised as a girl? Everyone in Binarowa laughed so hard that their stomachs ached.

Doctor, doctor, come here quick, because the cat is very sick. The cat could open doors with her paw and once ate some baby rabbits. Revenge will be fierce! They'll scald you in hell with boiling water and you'll give up the ghost like Grandad in the orchard full of apple trees, when he was pilfering fruit from the people who had long since stopped looking, because under water you can't see clearly. And whoosh, cat in the hot saucepan. And whoosh, pitchfork on the cat's back. Granny tied the cat up with red ribbons, the same she used for Bay and me. Then she watched to see if they formed signs in the wind, the signs her friend sent her; the one who didn't want to get on the train. When the ribbons fluttered to the left: hand over your crayons, to the right: raus/get out, upwards: pull down your pants, downwards: on your knees. Granny rehearsed these merry twists and swirls in the field.

Hooray, hooray, it's Saturday, we'll be drowning a cat today. Washtub in the kitchen all morning basking in the sun, the water will be warm. Mama's bustling around the house, frying crackling, wiping the dust from the panelling, the chicks have a light on even during the day, because the meat tastes better when heated. The fat melts more easily and you can lick your fingers after. Me and my little brother like to lick our fingers. Especially when Granny brings bananas. Before she reaches the barn, she takes them from her bag and measures which one is bigger. Right hand for little brother, left for Anielka. The one in the right hand is always as big as a machine gun. My brother runs in circles around Grandma and tells her to fall on the floor. Gun-gun-gun, hit Grandma in the lung! And she kneels before my little brother and cries: "Never again the crayons. I'll give them back to you, I'll put them outside the barn, come, Ester, for the crayons! I'll leave you all the colours, I didn't draw anything, I didn't chew any. Come, Ester, at dusk, I'll give you back the drawing you gave me when you got on the train."

When he was alive, Grandad would take Grandma by the armpits and lead her to the barn. There, on the hay bales, he knocked out of her mind the coloured crayons, the large rifle barrels, and little Ester, who drew the best pictures in school. And the crickets are already drowning in the washtub. What a shame, because in the evening we collect them in a jar. They play a concerto for five violins, two cellos and a double bass. And you don't have to pay for it, not like the merry-go-round that came to Gorlice. I only went on a horse there once, when Grandma sold two pounds of cherries. Three minutes and it was time to get off, but the little horse kept spinning and shouting: "Giddy up, giddy up, whee! Little girl, come to me! I'll take you to faraway lands where crocodiles eat dates, and wasps like coconuts."

And the little horse span and winked and shook its mane.

"Like it's alive," said Grandma.

You could make Bay look like that, colour in with a crayon here, attach a bow there, paint his lips and he'd be ready. But Bay did not want to be made-up. "Poor horse can barely breathe now," Grandad said.

He spurred him on with a whip, kicked him with his boots, braided his tail, and drove him off to the field for potatoes.

"Let that bloody horse die on the road, not while he's

scoffing oats," Grandad used to say when he was angry at Bay for floundering again.

Oh, a beetle with a dark green shell has drowned in the bathtub too, and the wasp that was trying to fly up our noses. We don't like wasps because Stasiu got stung by them once and he's been lying for three years on cemetery hill, next to the aunt who buried the jar of gold. His mama cried so hard when the other mamas hung washed nappies, tiny hats and stained bibs outside their houses. Stasiu won't get anything dirty anymore, because all his things are dirty with earth. Stasiu won't eat anything because the earth has clogged his mouth. Stasiu, Stasiu, aren't you missing your mama who howls like our Mongrel at night when she can't sleep? Stasiu, Stasiu, aren't you missing your papa, who's lying with ours in a ditch and digging for you with his hands? But Stasiu says nothing now, just sometimes at night he whimpers when the crickets end their concerto for five violins, two cellos and a double bass.

Saturday, drowning the cat today. First, I, Anielka, will jump into the washtub, because I am the youngest and I lick my fingers the best. Daddy's fingers are always glistening when he's finished skinning a chick, and I clean the bones and lick my fingers thoroughly. Mama pours water over our heads and washes our hair with nettle shampoo, which sends huge snowdrifts falling from our heads. She always holds me underwater and my brother counts to thirty. Sometimes he loses count and starts again, but Mummy never lets me go. Mummy toughens us up, because when we go out into the world, we must be able to fill our lungs with water and not make a sound. Mummy likes it when we wave our arms and the bubbles go up. She says she saw bubbles like that in the swamp, when a fox was drowning and its red tail was sticking up. So she shows Daddy the bubbles, saying: "Come here, I'll show you bubbles that go up, like that fox when it was drowning in the swamp. Come here now, because the fox is naughty, it's lowering its tail and the bubbles are disappearing."

Daddy comes into the kitchen, puts down the axe and pulls Mummy by the hair.

"There's no fox here, that's our Anielka, she's got golden hair that shimmers like rust in the sun. When you tie it in a ponytail, she looks like a fox, but this is our Anielka, our only daughter, filling her lungs with water and not making a sound."

Mummy lowers her head and Daddy pauses over the washtub. I like it when Daddy stands over the washtub, because he also lets the crickets bathe. Their instruments always get wet and they stop playing. Grandma, on the other hand, doesn't like to take a bath. She goes last and she gets into the washtub in her dress. No one else has to take a bath after Grandma, because she's the last one, and by that time the water is like the sour rye soup with sausage that we cooked for Mateuszek's communion. But when my uncle comes into the kitchen, when I'm taking a bath with the crickets and Papa's standing over the tub, I want to drown. May the fires of hell consume me, like that cat that ate the little rabbits. May my uncle turn into a ghost that frightens children over the swamps. May he go blind like Granny, who no longer recognises little Ester's drawing. But my uncle does not become a ghost, he can see everything and he says that he's found a foal in the field.

"Dunno whose it is," he says. "I'll raise it and sell it."

Or it'll be for leather, like Bay, who died in the stable while he was scoffing oats, I think. My uncle never lay in the ditch with Papa, because he's always practising Hosanna in the evenings; he can't play anything else. Not like my crickets.

Papa in the ditch, and today's Friday, and we need to fetch sugar from Pani Owczarowa, who is still alive, because she pilfers sausage and lard from her granddaughter Dorotka, and gives her crusts of bread with margarine to lick. Dorotka is my friend and she lives in the house lower down, but she's not as pretty as the Virgin Mary and she doesn't have a crown on her head, she stinks like Mongrel, who likes to roll around in the liquid manure when Mama takes it out and pours it on the currants so they'll bear plenty of fruit and so I can ride on my bicycle and sell them to Pani Zofia, Pani Hanna and Pani Maria. On Friday, the panelling is gleaming, because Mama's been wiping it all day; bit by bit, little by little, every hour, every hour, and it glistens like the dog lard that you have to drink when your lungs are sick. A teaspoon of sweetened tea, two teaspoons of lard, pinch your nose, bottoms up. The lard dissolves under your tongue, and you're healed. We got the lard in Rożnowice for six pounds of cherries. Granny says that over at number thirty-four, they eat dogs with potatoes and salad for dinner. We would never eat Mongrel, because he can sing opera arias with Stasiu's mother. He's a real singer, like Pavarotti, that Mongrel, and you wouldn't get any lard from him anyway. My brother and I counted his ribs, because he's so skinny and he doesn't want to eat anymore, he just sneezes and sneezes all the time and hides in his kennel when Papa throws him bones. Today Papa won't fetch sugar from Pani Owczarowa or throw bones to Mongrel, although he has on his Sunday socks and the shoes he wears for name days. He's still lying in the ditch, but he's not digging with his hands like Stasiu's father, who goes looking for his son at night. Papa's been lying in the ditch for four days now, and Mama isn't going to get him because her finger and head hurt. Any old excuse. Mummy secretly told Granny that Papa could go ahead and die. Papa can go ahead and die like Bay, who for twelve days didn't drink water or eat oats. Grandad speared him with a pitchfork and then cried for a long time, because there was no one to bring potatoes. Or maybe he was crying for Bay, he was just ashamed in front of Grandma, because he'd told her that when she was dead, he wouldn't shed a tear. Grandma didn't cry at Grandad's funeral either, although she'd said that when Grandad died, she'd throw herself in the River Sitniczanka. Splash, straight into the water. "Don't save me!" she would cry, and she'd sink straight to the bottom, where the pikes would gnaw at her feet and hands. But Granny didn't cry when Grandad gave up the ghost in the orchard full of apple trees, because a few weeks later, Franz was already plucking feathers for new pillows and putting ventilation in Grandma's hall so the Virgin Mary in Grandma's picture wouldn't rot and her crown could shine.

On Fridays, Mummy boils sugar with water and adds alcohol, which Granny hides in the stable. From early morning, my little brother and I are washing bottles and tearing off the colourful labels. It's a pity little Ester isn't here, she would draw new ones. For Pan Andrzej from the forest, it would have birds on, because he likes to rip open their bellies and put in artificial eyes in place of the real ones. For Pan Władek it would have a vat of tar, because when he gets angry at his wife, he shouts that she'll burn like the ones who went on a trip. For Pani Marta from across the river, it would be the singer Irena Santor, because she likes watching her on TV, how she twists her lips when she sings sad songs. Pani Marta turns on the TV and sings There Are No More Wild Beaches with Irena, although she's never been to the beach herself and never collected amber, only a Colorado beetle in potatoes in exchange for one little bottle of spirit with sugar. No drawings for Papa, because he hasn't got up yet and he hasn't said what he'd like drawn. Mummy will sell a few bottles and we'll buy new slippers with colourful patterns. Not for Papa, because until he gets up, he can't try them on, so they won't go to waste. We could also buy new tights, brighter than Kasia's, but first on the bicycle to Pani Hanna, Pani Maria and Pani Zofia, who doesn't have any children, because her fiancé died a long time ago. But Pani Zofia doesn't howl at night like Mongrel and Stasiu's mother, because she can't speak. That's what happened to her when they told her that her fiancé wasn't coming back, because one day he went to sleep and he never woke up – so says Grandma. Since then, she only walks in the fields at night and stretches her arms up to the sky, she opens her mouth, but she won't say anything. And that's why Grandma's Lord God can't answer her prayers, because He doesn't know why she's knocking on His door when she stretches out her hands and stands on tiptoe. And that aunt who's lying with Stasiu on cemetery hill, she died at the hands of Grandma's Lord God, that's what Mama used to say. I just don't know if it was the one with the short beard or the one with the long beard, and whether there was lightning, or maybe angels were flying overhead. Me and my little brother, when there's a storm, we go out into the meadow and stretch our hands up to the sky. Take us, Lord God. Send us rain, let it extinguish what Grandad set alight. Let Papa get up from the ditch, although he hasn't got up in his new socks and shoes for four days now. Let Mama give the new panelling back to the redheads, because it hasn't gone black yet, and they'll have something nice to come home to. They will wipe it with a cloth every day, Mama, like you. Let them have some spirit in clean bottles. We'll make them labels with colourful lights to guide them back home. Let Grandma give the drawing back to little Ester, who's giving her the signal that she's boarded the train. Let Mateuszek not die, although I told him in anger that he should die when he chopped off a piece of Mongrel's tail with an axe. Let the next pig not hang like Saint Andrew, but go to distant countries where crocodiles like dates, and wasps like coconuts. Let the horse on the merry-go-round spin not for three minutes for two pounds of cherries, but for fifteen minutes. Let Bay scoff a lot of oats and take Grandpa to get potatoes, because it's time to harvest, take out the manure and spread it in the fields. Let Papa get up, go to church or bathe in the washtub. Let Mama forget the fox that drowned in the swamps, and not make my little brother count to thirty. Let Grandma dig out from under the currants the five rings, three silver-plated rosaries, three communion rosaries, one signet ring and a gemstone – a sapphire, supposedly, because it shone deep blue – and return them to whoever my aunt stole them from. Maybe then they'd give her mouth-to-mouth and my aunt could help Grandma milk the cows. Let Kazio not lie like a mummy, but flit up high like a ladybird, and let Stasiu's mother go into the ground with Stasiu, because he's cold there and he wants some milk. Let the Virgin Mary's crown in Grandma's picture shine, then along with Grandad she will light the way to Papa, who hasn't got up for four days. Let Pani Zofia stretch her arms to the sky with us and stop fearing the lightning, although the fear is as large as a house.

Wintering

Mira is six when she walks in the dark for the first time. The snow creaks and sticks to her boots. I wish I were deaf, she thinks. The milk churn feels heavier than usual. She's limping on her right leg. Her heart is like that of a thrashing bird. Mira has seen one of those before. Andrzej, who lives near the forest, caught a lesser spotted eagle. Every morning, he took it outside his hut and tied it with a green shoelace to the handle of the brass tub. Mira had seen a lace like that before, on calfskin boots. The bird's leg was injured because it kept pecking at the knot and trying to fly away. In the winter, it left red stains in the snow.

"This bird's feathers stink," Andrzej had once said.

"My hair stinks," says Mira now.

A small stream of smoke is rising from the chimneys. It'll go up to heaven and never return, thinks Mira. The snow reminds her of a large, ironed sheet that she would like to hide her head under. Her shorter leg slows her down even more when she tries to run. Milk spills from the churn.

"Bring coal," says Konieczny to his wife.

The woman takes the basin from the kitchen. In front of the house, she tips out the suds left over after bathing. Steam rises from the snow, leaving a hole. Like acid eating away at skin, the woman thinks. She pours six full shovelfuls into the coal scuttle. She dips her hands in and licks them.

"I've got a black tongue," she says quietly to herself.

She walks slowly, leaning to the right. In the snow she leaves dark tracks.

"I had a dream. I was walking through the fields in winter. It was quiet, all I could hear was my own footsteps on the frozen snow. The birds had their beaks open, but they didn't make a sound. The trees stood motionless. Right next to the forest I passed our little one, she was spilling milk from the churn. She had tiny icicles on her eyelashes. She was limping and trying to run. I wanted to shout after her, but my voice didn't come out," says Konieczny's wife.

With her bony fingers, she lifts her blouse and puts the baby to her breast. Her nipples are purple, the skin is white, blue veins forming a thick spider's web. The baby eats ravenously. She's chomping like a puppy on a bitch, thinks Konieczny. The woman dips her free hand into a basket of buttons. She can't find the red one with the gold rim.

"Magda's jumper is missing a red button. Can you help me find one?" she asks.

Konieczny gets up from the table and rummages in the small wicker basket with his dirty hands. He touches his wife's milk-engorged breast and begins to suck. The baby is still awake. Konieczny's wife carries her over to the cot.

"Wake up tomorrow. Don't forget about me," she whispers.

The baby smiles. She reminds Konieczny's wife of a clay figure she made as a child. The woman takes off her tights, skirt, blouse, knickers and bra. She stands facing the wall.

"Closer," says her husband.

She spreads her legs wide. Her husband's fingers tug at her nipples. Too dry, thinks Konieczny.

There's a lot of snow this year. People sink into it up to their waists. It is caked on their clothes. They squint against the brightness. If someone were to sink into it completely, they wouldn't be dug out until it thawed. Their right or left arm would be raised high. Eyes and ears open. Boots tied. The trees bow towards the ground.

Andrzej hardly ever comes to the village in winter. He has everything he needs: buckwheat, potatoes, a supply of cigarettes and matches, sausage, pickled cucumbers. There's a Złotnicka White sow in the pigsty, a Saanen goat and a small Jersey cow the colour of a roe deer in the cowshed. The cow produces a creamy, yellowish milk. Andrzej likes fatty meat and creamy milk the most. In three months, I'll bring the Złotnicka out, he thinks. The snow will melt and then I'll slit her throat.

In Andrzej's hut there's a bed, a table and two chairs, two pictures hanging on opposite walls. One of them depicts a Polish hound. It has brown fur, and a pheasant in its mouth. The eyes of the bird are a dull white. The dog is raising its left paw. In the picture by the window, children are walking home from school. The sun is setting, emitting a pink glow. The children look like porcelain dolls. Andrzej stares at the picture. She won't show up today, he thinks. In the corner of the room lies a dried bird waiting to be stuffed. Its feathers are still shiny. Andrzej goes out in front of the hut. He stares into the night for a long time. He feels that the darkness is penetrating the walls. If I screamed, would the darkness bolt like a wild animal? he wonders. He is holding a rope.

Before going to bed, Konieczny's eldest daughter braids her hair into a long, blonde plait. I won't show up today, she thinks. Through the half-open door, she watches her mother standing by the wall. My hair is thicker, she thinks.

"When I stare at the mirror for a long time, I'm not sure if it's me," she says quietly to her little sister.

Konieczny's eldest daughter strips naked.

She stands in front of her sister, facing to one side.

"You can hardly see it," says the younger girl.

The older girl's breasts are perky with big pink nipples. She bows her head slightly and licks her left breast. A small trickle runs down her leg. He'll have to take the bird out, she thinks with a shudder, I don't like it when it's looking at me.

The frost came at night. It settled on the windows, leaving imprinted patterns. Most of the dogs are still sleeping in their kennels. Only some of them stick their muzzles out. Their eyes are cloudy. They want to go back to sleep. You can hear every sound at this time of day. The sound of a chain beating against a kennel carries all the way to the edge of the village. Konieczny's dog is up already, the milkman thinks, harnessing his horse.

Konieczny's dog stands in front of the kennel, cowering as if before a blow.

Today I'll finish my rounds quicker and stop by to see Konieczny's eldest, the milkman thinks. I'll pour a little from each churn and give it to her. Maybe she won't flinch this time? The milkman's horse won't leave the stable. She gets a couple of whips on her worn-out flank. The man touches the marks left by the blows. Her skin must be so delicate in those places too, he thinks. The horse walks slowly. The milkman dozes off. He wrenches himself from his dream, and returns to it again. The horse stops near the first farmyard and whinnies.

"I'd be lost without you," he says to the animal and bends down to get the milk churns.

Finally, the cart passes Konieczny's house. The dog raises its muzzle and looks at the sky. The Nysa police van is parked under a frost-distorted apple tree. There will be drinking and fucking. I won't stop by today, the milkman thinks.

Andrzej awakens, freezing cold. For a long time he doesn't open his eyes. I won't light the stove, he decides. He slowly sits up in bed. He picks up a pack of cigarettes from the side table, takes a heavy drag. Looks at the windows. If I were a painter, I would paint frosted feathers, he thinks. Then he buries his head in his hands and cries.

He goes out in front of the hut. The dog wags its tail when it sees him. It paws at the bowl of frozen water. Andrzej sees the cart in the distance. The milkman looks like a puppet operated by the wind. Andrzej takes the thick rope from his pocket. He wraps it round his hand. I'll bring the cow out first, that'll be the quietest, he thinks.

With the rope around his hand, he enters the cowshed.

"What time did she leave home?" the first policeman asks Konieczny.

The first policeman has thick fingers and short fingernails. His uniform is deep blue, like bunches of ripe grapes. Konieczny brings his hands up to his face, as if shielding his eyes from the sun. The first policeman pokes him with his truncheon.

"We're not on a social call today," he says.

"It was nighttime when she went out. She wanted to see if the snow shone in the dark," says Konieczny.

"She wanted to see if snow in the dark is whiter," says Konieczny's wife.

She's pouting like mine does when she takes it in her mouth, thinks the second policeman.

"And you weren't afraid to let such a little girl out in the dark?" he asks.

"I went out when I was even younger," replies Konieczny's wife.

"Which leg was she limping on?" asks the first policeman.

"The right. When she was born, it wasn't visible straight away. I didn't know what to look for," says Konieczny's wife. "Did the frost paint lovely patterns on your windows too?" she asks after a moment.

Konieczny's wife's eyes soften again.

"We'll drive around and look for her. If she's fallen into a snowdrift, she won't be dug out until it thaws. The snow has covered all the tracks," explains the first policeman.

Konieczny and his wife don't get up to say goodbye. They look at their hands lying on the table. Konieczny's wife's nails are long and cream-coloured. How does she caress with those nails? the second policeman wonders.

Konieczny's eldest daughter puts on a thick sheepskin coat over her nightgown. She won't have time to undo her plait.

"Don't say where I went. Let them think that I've gone out to look for her," she begs her younger sister.

Her cheeks are red from the cold. She walks faster and faster and stumbles more and more. The thin skin on her legs begins to burn, her nipples stiffen. It's so quiet that the crashing of felled trees can be heard from the end of the village. Birds hide among the dry, bare branches. Down by the chapel, she sees the sleeping milkman. The horse is slowly pulling the cart of full milk churns. Each churn has the name of its owner written on the side. Just like in the cemetery, we've all got someone there, thinks Konieczny's eldest daughter. When she looks back, the milkman is swaying from side to side. The horse lurches ahead as the icy wind picks up.

Konieczny's eldest daughter sees traces of blood in the snow. He was going to bring the Złotnicka out in three months and only then slit her throat, she recalls. She enters the hut and creeps about quietly. There's no bird in the corner.

"I'll be able to come here more often. That bird stank," she says out loud.

She reaches into her coat pocket and takes out a small red button with a gold rim. The door to the cowshed is wide open.

Zofia

I told them, "Life isn't kind to me," and I stood on my tiptoes and began to twist the invisible knot above my head, tying it like shoelaces. I'd done those knots so many times, and standing on my toes, and the sure, slow movements around my neck, so that the rope will hold when I want it to. I'd go out behind the house, into the woods, to the barn, and start the ballet. First, I'd practise standing as high as I could for as long as I could, and that hurt the most, and only after that, with my arms above my head. You have to stay on your toes as long as possible, cos when the whole foot touches the ground again, it starts walking. The heart wants to stay with the hands in the air but the legs are rushing forwards. It was like that before the storm too – I was flying as fast as an arrow and suddenly I dropped the handkerchief my mother had given me. She'd embroidered a small sunflower on it and when I left the house she always asked, "Zofia, where's your hanky?"

I'd pull out my pockets and say: "Look, here, I'll never lose it."

And when I turned around, I saw the handkerchief lying in the road, but my legs couldn't stop for fear.

"Holy Mother, the wolf from the forest, the intercessor, the cow in calf and without calf, Jesus drinking honey from the hive, the fox with the injured tail, go with us through the world." That's what I said when the village started to burn.

And the day before that, I dreamed that my mother was sitting in the kitchen cooking soup. So I said to her, "Mummy, if you're dead, do you still remember all the recipes?"

But my mother didn't answer me, and I thought she couldn't hear me, so I called even louder: "Mummy, if you're dead, do you still remember all the recipes?"

After a while she came over to me and, just like when I was little, she blindfolded me, led me to the table and gave me various things. And I told her: wood, sugar, flour, mushroom, apple, dog, bee, corn stalk, wheat, cat, chicken leg, until I felt something burning under my fingers. I ripped off the blindfold, but I couldn't see anything, there was darkness before my eyes, and suddenly my clothes caught fire.

"That's how I dreamt up your fire," I told the neighbours whose house burnt down, taking with it three cows, five pigs, twenty chickens, eighteen ducks, the older girl Eleonora and little Helenka.

And a few weeks after that dream, Franek came to me at night, clean, in a white shirt and trousers with creases, and told me how he was looking for the little girl.

"But I didn't find her, she must have turned to ashes, cos no one who entered the cottage could see her anywhere. I only saw the older one, Eleonora, sitting by the window, all charred. I walked through the embers, I looked in every corner, but nothing. So I took the older one, carried her out in my arms, I was afraid she'd break in half, she was so burnt. I carried her like a bride over the threshold, but I had to be careful, cos what kind of wedding day would it be if she was missing an arm or leg? But I'm marrying you anyway," Franek promised me.

After that promise, when I woke up every morning, I'd just be waiting for the day to turn to evening, cos then I could run to meet Franek in the place we'd agreed. Only the first thing I did was pick up a stick to chase the kids with, cos sometimes they barred my way.

"Where you off to, then?" they'd ask. "Your fiancé ain't waiting for you nowhere, cos his head's covered with earth. Your fiancé won't take your hand, cos his fingers were eaten by creepy-crawlies, look, like these!" And they'd throw earwigs, ants and beetles at my head.

I'd brush off the bugs and tread them into the ground with my shoes, then I'd wave my stick at the little brats and swing it about until it whacked one of them in the knees, head or back.

"Get away, get away! May everything that's born to you rest in a dark grave before it opens its eyes, may your mothers and fathers disown you not three times but thirty, may the dead rise from their graves and set fire to everything that's dear to you in this world."

And when they spat on me, I didn't wipe my face, I just bellowed so loud that the earth cracked in half, and when the earth cracked and they saw there was nothing inside, they ran away, even more afraid than if they'd seen raging flames. And I could stand tall and go to meet Franek at the place we'd agreed, and he was almost always waiting for me like I was a queen.

But sometimes I was the one waiting, and then I'd watch

vigilantly like a dog, and when I finally caught a glimpse, it would take a moment before I knew it was Franek, cos he'd be wearing a thick sheepskin coat, a hat made of rabbit fur that I'd given him, and he'd be dragging his right leg behind him like someone that wasn't him.

"Are you ill or something? The sun's out, and you're dressed like that?" I asked, but Franek was speaking less and less, often only one word, and so quietly that I didn't understand what it was.

It's because of the leg, I thought, when something hurts, you don't feel like eating or talking. I kept having to wait longer and longer for him, and sometimes he wouldn't come at all. But when he didn't come, I'd wait anyway, then I'd get up and go to his house to stare at the windows, and I'd stare so long I'd think I was about to go blind, but I'd never turn my head away, cos what if he flashed past and I didn't notice? I knocked on his door only once, but I regretted it right away, cos his father came at me with boiling water.

"If you want, you little tramp, you can go to cemetery hill in Rożnowice, if you dig around a bit you'll find Franek there."

"We didn't arrange to meet on the hill," I told him. "He was meant to meet me, but he didn't come."

I went to all the places we'd been together, and everywhere I carved a heart in the earth with a stick as a sign that I'd been there. So if he came to the brook instead of the forest, he'd know right away that I hadn't forgotten. And that's when, out of the boredom of waiting, or from longing for him, I started to stand on my tiptoes and practise. At first nothing came of it, I fell to the ground right away, the knots turned to loops and I had to raise my hands and untangle them.

"These dances are no use to me," I said, but after a while I was able to stay on my feet for longer, and my hands moved more ably.

And when I was standing tall, though I don't know how many months had passed, I saw that Franek was finally coming. But is that Franek? I thought, as he got closer. He was dragging his leg even more and was bent over like our sexton when he's lighting the candles on the altar on Sundays, who's so hunched already that his hands nearly hang to the floor. He grovels before God, and Franek grovels before me – that's what came to mind.

"Where've you been, what were you doing, why haven't I seen you? I followed you at night, stood for hours outside your house, and it was like the earth had swallowed you up. Tell me right now, where the hell were you, did you run off to marry that girl from the fire, the one you carried over the threshold like a bride? Look me in the eye right now and tell me, as you promised you would."

"I've been here the whole time, dear Zofia. I watched you stand on tiptoe and raise your hands. Your fingers are well trained now, your arms are strong, your knots are sturdy, but do you hear their weeping? Do you hear them, Zofia? The little one whimpers so quietly, like she doesn't even want to be spotted, and the older one doesn't say a word, cos the lightning struck her in the throat, she points which way I should go, which corner I should check. And I run this way and that, but there's nothing there. Would you come with me and see, maybe she'll show you where the baby is?"

I stopped talking to my sisters and my father, I had no words left in my mouth, and when I tried to part my lips to say something, all that came out was aaaaaaaa, as if I was just learning to speak. Cos what would I say, to whom, and why? Franek didn't stick to his promise, he didn't come to our meeting places anymore, and the hearts that I drew on the ground with a stick got trampled by the kids.

"Show us, Zofia, what's under your frock, show us, Zofia, what's in your heart, and we'll tell you if any more fellas are coming your way," they teased me.

I just kept working and practising, practising, the same as always. Behind the house, near the forest, in the barn, so no one would see me. That day at noon, when we went to dig the hay, I whirled the rake around like I was chasing devils. Got to finish quickly and carry on practising, I thought. I watched Maria and Antek giggling, she wrote words in the air for him and he had to read them, and then she drew hearts for him, which peeved me the most, cos they were lopsided. So I threw down my rake and stood up straight in front of them, raised my arms as high as I could and began to make neat little knots in the air, strong enough to hold a bull.

"Life isn't kind to me," I told them.

I was knocked off balance by a rake blow to the back from my father, but I straightened up again and went back to twisting.

"Hit me in the head, in the back, it doesn't hurt, I'm waiting for someone to give me a proper walloping," I bawled as I saw the rake snap.

First the Hair Caught Fire

"The small grave over by the fence, there's nobody in there. There's no body, they never found it. They looked for it, but found nothing, not even a bone. No wonder, because they were far away, and the summer was that hot, if you threw a match everything went straight up in flames. The earth scorched, and the straw went so quick, it was over before you knew it. Just like life. You go to work or church, come back, and someone's lying with their arms spread out or their head bloodied. Or you don't come back at all, and the soup's steaming on the table, the dog's waiting by the road and doesn't notice it's suddenly gone dark. For me it went like this, I come home after work and I call out: 'Lucynka! Lucynka! Come and see, I've brought six pounds of cherries for juice.' And I stood there for a minute, because the whole house seemed somehow too quiet, and I felt this pang in my heart, like someone was clenching their fist round it with all their might. I dropped the cherries and ran straight to the kitchen, everything was set out ready for cooking, but the fire had almost gone out. She was lying in the corner of the smallest room, where it was darkest and coldest. She must have gone to the window and looked out towards Binarowa, as she often did. What's it like for other people? Everyone seems to have their own story, but somehow they're all similar. Anyway, I was meant to be talking about that grave. It's always been empty."

The bushes are sagging, heavy with raspberries. This year the fruits are so big that the buckets quickly fill to the brim. The raspberries grow opposite the house and when it's quiet, you can hear the buzzing of insects. It's a monotonous, muffled sound that lulls you into a deep and silent sleep, and when suddenly something snaps you out of it, you don't know if you're still on the side of sleep, or back in the real world. The sweet scent of raspberries mingles with the smell of the cherry trees that Eugeniusz planted many years ago. This fragrance, pleasant and mild, turns acrid and oppressive after a while. Maybe the heat sharpens the senses, and man becomes like a sniffing dog? But for now, the heat is slowly seeping in. It's six in the morning and the sun is shining brighter than usual. The night's dampness is evaporating off the cut hay, dew drops are vanishing from the plants. The silence is broken by the first brisk commands. Movement starts up in the house and barn. If you stood outside, it would be hard to tell whose voices they were. Every so often, a woman's song carries in the air.

Eleonora is sitting at the table, using a sharp knife to slice the tomatoes picked yesterday. Her short-cropped black hair gleams like a raven's wings. She is slim and tall. In a few days she'll turn thirteen. Before she slices into each tomato, she turns it in her hand and sniffs, as if she feels sorry to be breaking the delicate, reddened skin. She smiles, but no one sees. Everyone is busy getting ready to go the field. The hay has dried and they need to start digging before the swelter of August turns into the waning heat of September. Prior to leaving for work, everyone is restless. They hurriedly search for rakes and pitchforks, carelessly cut the bread and stuff pieces of pork fat between the slices.

"Eleonora, go to the well and pour some water into the churns," says Mother and takes little Helenka, who smiles at the sight of her, from the cradle.

"Alright," replies Eleonora and out she goes.

She slouches like her father, her mother thinks. I hope she grows out of it. She pulls up her blouse and puts the baby to her breast. The little one nurses slowly, pausing every now and then to stare at her mother's face. Before long, the woman carries the baby over to the cradle and hands her a rag doll. Eleonora stands by the window and watches her family leave. After a while they become little dots fading into the distance. Her mother's long, dark plait blends into the background, and it's hard to tell if the figure is still a woman. She can't see the wide hips that sway most beautifully in summer dresses, or the strong, tanned legs and arms. It seems to Eleonora that the world ends just beyond the horizon. She turns her gaze to the apple tree and the shade beneath it. The leaves aren't moving, no birds are taking refuge among its branches. It's so quiet that she's afraid to say a word. She feels that if even one long, melodious aaaaaaaaaaa were to come out of her mouth now, the glass in the windows would break, the desiccated roof over the well would crumble to dust, and the raspberry bushes would slump to the ground like after a heavy downpour.

She stands still and her legs begin to tremble. If I followed them there, what would I see? she wonders. She recalls a frosty

November morning when she and her mother had gone to clean at the church. Her mother disappeared into the grey dawn on her bicycle, and Eleonora had forgotten her gloves, her fingers were stiffening, she could barely keep hold of the handlebars. Even though she was wearing her warmest jacket, the wind blew through her body and she couldn't catch her breath. Mother's left me, she thought, and tried to pedal faster and faster. Patches of snow lay on the roofs of the houses, and the barely frozen ground began to gleam with the first rays of the sun. Eleonora looked at the farms she passed, but not a single light bulb was on anywhere, no smoke rose from the chimneys, the kennels seemed to be uninhabited. She wanted to scream, but she was afraid – as she was now, standing in front of the window on that scorching hot morning, a bead of sweat running down her neck – that when the screaming stopped, she would see nothing but empty fields that had been stripped bare.

Her mother was kneeling with her back to her on the church floor and scraping off hardened wax with a scrubbing brush. Eleonora thought that when her mother turned around, she would have the face of one of the saints praying in the pictures that hung in the side aisle. A wet rag hit her in the chest.

"What took you so long?" Her mother eyed her suspiciously. "Go to the sacristy and give everything a good scrubbing."

Eleonora blushes at the memory and bites her lip hard. She goes over to the cradle. The baby's skin is pink from the heat and her fists are clenched.

"Dream, dream," Eleonora whispers and touches Helenka's cheek, which resembles a firm fruit.

In the evening, when they return from the field, I'll go to Rożnowice for Mass, I'll go past his house and see if he's in, she thinks. And if he's not home, I'll find him in the church by the tabernacle, to the right of the priest and to the left of Saint Stephen. His dark hair will conceal his face, but I'll know right away that it's him. And no one will know that for the whole of Mass, I'm not praying to God, nor to Mary, nor to their child. I'll wear my white dress with small yellow flowers, I'll tie my hair with a red ribbon, I'll put my patent leather shoes on, no tights, and the moment he looks, I'll cross my legs. I'll be the first to go up for communion so that he'll remember who he held the paten for first, and when the priest crosses himself for the last time, and the people stop singing and the church empties out, I'll stay kneeling and see if he leaves his surplice in the sacristy. And when he's leaving, I'll give that dolt Julka the metal ring I found in the hay, get her to tell him that it's from me, that it's forever.

Eleonora sits down in the small room by the table, her eyes are closed. In the kitchen, next to the cradle where Helenka sleeps, a cat is playing with a small dead mouse. It is so quiet, you can hear its contented purrs and the thumping of its paws on the floorboards. The girl dreams of raspberry bushes and the buzzing of insects, which wakes her up. She opens her eyes and sees raindrops on the window, hears the first rumbles of thunder in the distance.

"I knew it was coming," she says.

"People have asked who noticed the fire first. The mother, the father? But who remembers things like that after all these years? No one knows how fast they ran, whose legs carried them further, but whoever you ask, they'll all say the same: the glow rose over the whole valley and everyone was walking round like they were blinded. All I'll say is the two of them entered the house, and the ceiling was almost caved in. The older one, Eleonora, she was carried out by some lad, I don't remember his name. Only he must have gazed at her too deeply, because a few weeks later he died in his sleep, and he was healthy, nothing wrong with him. The thing about the dead is that it's better when they're at a distance, because later they come for us and there's no turning back. But when he went inside, she was sitting at the table, by the open window. Probably a flash of lightning got her, like a stray bullet. But where she'd been hit is anyone's guess. It's a fairly quick death, because when lightning strikes, you probably don't feel a thing, or only for a moment. Isn't that what people think? I reckon the soul goes straight up to heaven, and the body disintegrates in the grave, because even the vermin won't touch a burnt corpse like that. The worst part is that little one, because no one ever found her and there are some who think they hear her crying at night. Everyone says the little angel must have been sleeping and didn't even feel a thing, but between you and me, the stench was unbearable, like five piglets had been seared alive over the fire. Anyway, they told me to dig this grave, so I dug it and put up a plaque with the inscription: In eternal memory of Helenka Płaczek."

On Cemetery Hill

The girl is still asleep, her fists are clenched. A trickle of saliva runs down from her mouth, but it soaks into the pillow and there won't be any embarrassing marks when she wakes up. The girl is lying on her stomach. Her rolled up nightgown reveals skin slightly darkened by the spring sun, smooth and taut on her buttocks and thighs; her small feet hang limply. Her long, blonde hair is tangled like a boxful of yarn. Her lips are parted, her small, straight teeth visible, her tongue motionless. Andrzej crouches by the bed and turns her onto her back. He touches her small breasts and pink nipples, then stands and looks down at her.

Andrzej wakes up.

He has this dream almost every night, sometimes the girl wakes up, but after a while her eyes glaze over, she stops blinking. Andrzej would like to shake her body, or even slap her, first only on the cheek, but if that didn't work, he would clamp his hands around her neck until she looked at him. He makes some random movements in the air, loses feeling in his arms and legs. After a while, he realises he's lying in his bed, barely covered by the blanket, it's the start of April. At this time of year, the earth is still softened from the snow, and it will be three months until it turns into hard clods. There will be long, hot days and warm evenings that will quickly strip moisture from plants, animals and humans.

"The earth is like an old whore. Once it closes up, nothing can get in," Cieniawa used to say.

Andrzej remembers these words as he rolls over onto his left side and tries to fall back to sleep, although he knows he's awake now. He hears drops of water falling into the bucket he left out in the kitchen. The roof has been leaking since his mother died. Two years have passed, and he puts the bucket in the same place every night. Before he gets up, he runs his fingers over the tattered wall-hanging beside the bed and presses his body against it. He stares at the orange thread that once, if he remembers correctly, was blood red. Now the colour resembles that of a big moon covered in soot. He would like to pull the thread and see how far the fabric unravels, but his index finger only moves slowly up and down, as if gently caressing the air. Andrzej's hands are strong, his deep blue eyes misty.

"When he looks people in the eye, it's like he's looking over their heads, far into the distance," his mother used to say.

Andrzej dons trousers and a denim shirt, his body is slim. The swelling on his face hasn't subsided yet. He leans towards the mirror and sweeps his beautiful, dark hair off his forehead.

It's a Saturday, early morning. Andrzej walks all around the house, trying to find the poppy-print scarf he once gave his sister.

She probably took it somewhere and forgot it, lost it, it's

gone. I'm not going to buy her anything else, he thinks, she just loses everything or trades it for any old rubbish. Henia and her daughter moved out three months ago, he's only seen them once since then. I'll have to take out their beds, no one's going to be sleeping there anymore, he thinks. He pushes his mother's bed aside, throws the dirty pillows on the floor, finds the poppy-print scarf under one of them, wraps it around his hand like a bandage, and goes outside. What did Mother want with this scarf? Or maybe Dorotka hid it? he wonders. He unwraps the colourful material, takes some matches from his pocket, and sets it alight. Then he brings the pillows, quilts, blankets and mattresses from the house, pours petrol over them and tosses another match on the pile. The fire chars the willow branches. Andrzej runs into the house and looks around for anything else he can add to the fire, he tosses his mother's clothes from the wardrobe onto the floor, the worn-out housecoats, underwear and a few dresses, among the clothes he finds a wad of old banknotes and a photo of his father standing on the shore of a lake wearing just swimming trunks and oversized glasses, his arms at his sides. What did she see in him? he wonders. He scoops it all up and takes it out, throws the photo on the pile last. He sits down near the house and looks at the fire, the dog tied to its kennel starts wagging its tail and barking. Andrzej lets it off the chain. The dog does a few quick laps of the house, runs up to him, puts its muzzle on his lap and looks him in the eye.

"There's nothing left for you here, run away," he says, but the animal doesn't budge. "Go on, off you go!" he says louder.

Finally, he gets up and throws a stone at the dog. The animal moves back a few yards and puts its head between its paws. Andrzej goes to the shed and looks for an axe, with a few swings he dismantles the bed where his mother and

Dorotka slept, and then his sister's sofa bed. Every few minutes he throws another large piece of wood on the fire. He keeps at it until late afternoon, wet from sweat and the heat. Then he just rinses off his face and goes out. The dog returns to its spot by the kennel and falls asleep.

At this time of day, the villagers begin to seek rest. Workworn women step out from their houses and sit on benches. In warm jumpers, with scarves over their heads, they take their knitting needles and yarn, or they fold their arms on their chests and look at the sky as if tempted to shake their fists at it. After a while, they fall asleep, soothed by the first warm rays. Approaching their houses, you can smell the duck broth and the sweet, delicate aroma of forsythia. The housewives' bodies are heavy, swollen and sore. They look like balloons that can't get off the ground. If you popped them, first bile would pour out of them, hidden all their lives beneath the heart, and then salt water.

On Saturday afternoon, when Andrzej is walking through the village, the girls are carefully washing their hair. In the daylight, the drops of water shimmer on their skin just as they do on the petals and stems of plants in the morning. On Saturdays, the girls work faster than usual and keep one eye on the clock. Since morning, the men have been turning away and sneaking sips of alcohol from bottles hidden in their waistbands, shamefully wiping beads of sweat on checkered handkerchiefs. When it starts to get dark, they will head towards cemetery hill and stop in at Finesse bar, lured by the glow of the Christmas lights that the owner has hung in the windows and under the ceiling. The housewives sitting on benches will be roused by the evening chill, for a moment they won't be able to tell whether they're awake or still asleep. They will rise and call to their children, and as they go up to the porch, they will check if their husbands' shoes are in the corner. Most will find an empty space, and polishing rags scattered about. They will bite their lips as they bend to pick up the dirty cloths. The blue light of the television will shine from the windows of each house, and the doors will stay open for the night.

At Finesse, there are several tables made of thin wooden planks, and wobbly chairs. You can order three drinks: beer, Fanta or Coca-Cola. If anyone's hungry, there are always a couple of zapiekanki in the freezer for the barmaid to pop into the grease-stained microwave for two minutes, then smother in ketchup. The radio behind the bar is on full volume, and in the other corner of the cosy room is a small TV; the sound hasn't worked for months, but it's always on anyway. The girls on the TV don't know they're dancing to the music from the radio, and they lose the rhythm every now and then. It's mostly men in the bar, they sit close together or stand by the walls, holding bottles of beer. The use of beer mugs was abandoned long ago because the barmaid couldn't keep up with sweeping the broken glass off the floor. The shards got stuck in the soles of shoes glistening with cheap polish and scratched the linoleum. Occasionally, a high-pitched giggle breaks out amidst the male laughter, but when it lasts too long it starts to resemble sobbing. Then everyone falls silent, and only when she is elbowed by her companions and suddenly goes quiet does the hubbub resume. The women usually only come to the bar one at a time: the militiaman's widow, Marta from over the hill, or Marta from across the river, for free drinks, and sometimes Zofia, searching for her dead fiancé.

Andrzej's place in the left-hand corner is taken by Edek, who also ran out of words after selling the last hectares of his orchard. More and more often he comes with a full bag of apples, slowly sips his beer and stares straight ahead as if he's admiring a white dolgo crabapple tree in bloom. Andrzej heads towards the window and notices that the table where he always sat with Piotrek and Pilot is still free. He hesitates, then sits down and touches the rough wooden planks. How many hands must have laid here before? he thinks. How many years have actually passed? He feels that every sip will be an effort today.

"What's on your mind, mate? We'll keep you company," says Wiesiek suddenly, pulling two chairs out from under the table. "Sit down," he tells the other man. "This is my brother-in-law, Zenek, don't think you've met."

Andrzej shrugs and looks at the TV.

The men sit in silence. Wiesiek plays with his lighter, flicking it and twisting it between his fingers. The brother-in-law sits upright, exhaling deeply after each sip of beer, as if in relief.

"Which one do you like best, Andrzej?" asks Wiesiek, staring at the girls in the music video, who are making tempting, inviting gestures with their hands. "I like the one in the middle. If she bent over, you'd see everything."

"What the fuck are you on about? The blonde one's the best," says the brother-in-law, suddenly animated. "I bet she's got the tightest pussy. Then again, you don't even know what a pussy looks like, so how could you compare," he adds with a cackle, choking on his cigarette smoke. "Unless you count that one you tried to drag into a ditch, but you've answered for that in the eyes of the law, and God – who either doesn't exist, or doesn't want to."

Wiesiek, without taking his eyes off the TV, repeats: "The one in the middle's the best. When she bends over, I'll see everything."

Andrzej closes his eyes. The girl wakes up and smiles.

"Come to me, just be quiet, let's not wake anyone," she whispers.

Andrzej lies down on the clean sheets, he's ashamed because he hasn't changed his clothes for four days. He turns onto his left side, the tapestry on the wall is bright red again. He finds a broken thread, tries to pull, but the fabric doesn't yield. The girl strokes his hair. "Leave it, or it'll unravel. It'll come away from the wall."

"Andrzej, what was the story with that bird you pulled out of the river at the last minute?" says Wiesiek suddenly, narrowing his eyes and taking a deep drag on his cigarette. "What was her name? Magda? Maryla? I can't remember for the life of me. Yonks ago, wasn't it? You can spill your guts now, like at confession. Cos apparently, she was up to her neck in water when you went in after her. What a hero, going in so deep! But people have short memories."

Andrzej slowly opens his eyes. The militiaman's widow is undoing more buttons on her blouse and pulling out a small green stone on a string from between her breasts.

"This is all I have left of him," she says to the men sitting around the table.

Everyone nods, but no one says a word. The barmaid is fixing her makeup and taking occasional sips of Coke through a straw. Wiesiek's brother-in-law stares motionless at the TV. The bar is getting stuffier and people are looking at each other with smoke-reddened eyes as if they've been crying.

"So, what happened? You went in after her, and then what?" asks Wiesiek, nudging Andrzej's shoulder. "They say she walked in with ten heavy stones in her dress. But would that many stones fit in two small pockets? She wasn't the fittest of the three, that's for sure. Did you know them?" he asks. "Now they're getting on a bit, but they're still not bad to look at, I'm not gonna lie. And that oldest one, apparently she knew foreign languages, went away to study, but clearly, it didn't sort her head out. I reckon someone fucked her and dumped her when she was living in the city, eh? You must've copped a feel, though, when you pulled her out of the river, yeah?" Wiesiek lowers his voice conspiratorially and winks at Andrzej. "Listen, and that sweetheart of yours, how old was she? Sixteen? Who wouldn't want to take a turn on a bird like that. But when they lost the youngest daughter, they stopped letting the others out of the house, your girl too, right? I knew straight away it wasn't your doing. I told everyone, but when people get an idea in their heads, there's no changing their minds! Only later they found her lying all the way over in Gorlice, undressed, face to the ground. Hard to believe someone could take a kid and... But she wasn't a kid, your girl. Sixteen years old, almost grown-up! It was the same with me, except they started dragging me through the courts and convincing her she hadn't wanted it. How the fuck did she not want it, when she lay down right next to me?!" He raises his voice and sets his bottle down heavily on the table. "But fine, I did my time, for all in the name of love, that's all it was. But to turn you from a hero into a villain? People just have poor memories, that's what it is. I wouldn't jump into a rushing river after some bird I didn't know. If she doesn't want to live, then be my guest, hey-ho, another one bites the dust."

Andrzej doesn't reply. He lights a cigarette and keeps staring at the TV.

"The priest doesn't like our Finesse, apparently," Wiesiek continues. "Says it's too close to the church, but mainly to the cemetery. I dunno what his problem is. I'd tell him straight, you can raise a glass with the dead too, yeah? On my way out of here, I often go to visit my folks up on cemetery hill. Do you go to visit yours? People say you don't even show up for All Souls' Day. Your mate Pilot's there too, right? And the other one's probably whizzing round in German cars, lucky bastard. Well, if he likes old biddies, go for it, that's not for me. Did you go to Pilot's funeral then, or not?"

Andrzej shakes his head.

"See? Even that. You have to say goodbye to the dead, or they'll follow you round like dogs."

The April nights are still cold. As Andrzej walks through the village, blue light flickers only in some houses, like a lantern flashing in the darkness. The housewives are sleeping with their mouths open and snoring softly, the children and dogs dream about their worries, and toss and turn in their beds and kennels. Andrzej stops outside Konieczny's house, takes the rope from his pocket and throws it over a branch of the tallest tree.

The Funeral

The sun rose very quickly, it was shaping up to be a muggy day. Sometimes heat emerges slowly, the plants hold on to their moisture, and the shade covers them lovingly. The world warms gradually, giving time to prepare. The coolness of the morning especially pleases the dogs, who roll about in the wet grass or the earth as if they think it will help them avoid the impending heat, the panting with their tongues out. But this day was different. It was immediately dry, the sun chased away the shade and scooped up everything it encountered on its way. Plants bowed towards the ground, leaves brushed the soil. The dogs roamed impatiently around their kennels, and those that ran loose searched for a patch of wet grass, or had been digging holes since dawn to get shelter for the rest of the day.

It will be muggy and quiet, Agnieszka thought as she walked out of the house barefoot and looked at the sky. The smell of the fire from a few days before still hung in the air.

"It will never go away," she said out loud to herself, shielding her face with her forearm, and she kept looking up.

After a while, she sat down on the grass and watched a wood ant that was carrying a wasp. The ant didn't seem to know where it was going: it reversed, went right, then suddenly turned left, then back and forth again. In the end, it headed for the blossoming hollyhock, where Agnieszka lost sight of it. She looked towards the house. It was large and beautiful. Green on the outside, with high windows in the porch, solid oak floorboards, the largest room painted a deep brown that reminded Agnieszka of the fur of a bear she'd seen on a postcard as a child. It was in this house, on loan from their neighbours who only came here for the holidays, that she would spend the next few months with Adam, until the winter, until their burnt-down house had been rebuilt.

She went inside and stopped outside the door to the largest room. Just a few days ago, she was filling the churns with water from the well, she thought, and turned the door handle.

"Will two be enough?" Adam asked. "I don't want to have to come in from the field."

"It should be. And I've told Eleonora to give cow's milk to Helenka, I don't want to be coming right back the moment we've left."

"Yeah, it'll take us a while. I don't know who's coming to help, they're digging over at the Jabłonowskis' today too."

"Oh well," said Agnieszka and touched her husband's shoulder. Her long plait reached down to her buttocks. "You didn't tie the dog up," she added suddenly, as the little rough-haired mongrel began to bark and mill about at her feet.

"Let him run free, I don't feel like chasing after him," he added, indifferent.

"As long as he doesn't get under the pitchfork!"

"Well, it's up to him whether he comes back with all his paws or not."

Every day since the fire, Agnieszka has replayed in her mind this conversation and the road they took. She wishes she could recall turning her head towards the house, but she can't locate the memory. The day had started as usual, they passed their neighbours and said hello, she took off her shoes because she liked to feel the earth and grass beneath her feet, but she soon put them back on, the earth was scorching, the grass was dry and prickly. When they arrived, Pilot was already waiting in the shade of a hazel tree, he was always the first to arrive and took a bottle of vodka in payment. The work went quickly, more neighbours came than they'd expected. Agnieszka could stack hay, although it was a job that required a lot of strength, women usually did the raking. Her father, despite the fact that he had two sons, had taken her to the fields from an early age. He used to wake her at dawn, and she never had the courage to refuse. No one said much while they were working, and they rarely took cigarette breaks, everyone wanted to finish as soon as possible and hide in the shade of the trees or a cool veranda. Agnieszka can't remember what she was thinking about as she quickly and deftly made stack after stack. During the only break, they all sat down in the tall grass, hazel branches hanging overhead. Agnieszka had known these trees since she was a child, they had always produced maggoty nuts. People would open a shell and curse and throw it on the ground. She only thought about Eleonora briefly, when Bartkowska asked if her daughter was going to Mass in Rożnowice.

"My Julka was saying all morning that she's going, the two

of them together, apparently. Like they're devout old ladies or something!" said Bartkowska, winking at Agnieszka.

"I don't know," Agnieszka replied, and for a moment she was angry that her daughter hadn't told her.

"Better they stare at boys in church than roll around with them in the bushes," said Bartkowska, struggling to her feet.

Agnieszka felt the first drops of rain on her skin.

"We have to hurry," she said loudly.

I didn't turn around for them, my daughters, thinks Agnieszka, standing in the cool interior of the green house. Even if I think about it endlessly, I can't see myself turning around. I walked on as if there was nothing behind me. All morning in a hurry, I put Helenka in her cradle too quickly, she must have been hungry, Eleonora was probably already thinking about the evening, but she didn't say a word. Did she try on her dress in front of the mirror? Which boy did she want to look her prettiest for? Maybe with all the excitement she didn't feed the baby on time? Or she forgot to cover her, and the rooms are cool in summer, even on days like that, when the sun eats into the bare earth.

Streaks of light enter the room through the treetops. Agnieszka stares at them, then goes to the wardrobe and takes out a long, black dress, tights and shoes. She licks her finger and wipes a small stain from the right shoe. She undresses and puts on her Sunday best. With a swift movement, she opens the wide white door to the room where two coffins have been placed, though one of them is empty. She can smell the sweet scent of the flowers scattered in every corner.

They'll be here soon, she thinks. Adam enters the room suddenly and touches Agnieszka's shoulder. The woman clenches her bandaged fists until red spots appear on the fabric.

It had started to rain sooner than she'd expected, but first it got muggy. The sun sank so low, it seemed everything around was about to burn, everyone was wringing their sweat-soaked shirts. Nobody broke the ensuing silence, they wanted to finish as soon as possible and escape from the field before the storm. Agnieszka looked at Bartkowska for a moment, the sweat was running down her forehead and cheeks, and between her breasts. Where will it end up? she thought. Bartkowska looked at her with a smile, as if she knew what she was thinking, but she didn't stop working. The sky was flooded with a thick, deep blue that was getting darker and darker, it seemed as if the air was turning black.

The first clap of thunder was powerful, followed by a sudden downpour, and everyone darted towards the nearest barn. Agnieszka ran slower. Like Eleonora, she wasn't afraid of storms. They always looked out of the window when a storm was on its way, and they stayed there until the sky was flooded with milk-white clouds. Each thunderclap made Agnieszka's heart beat faster – but not from fear. She felt excitement, as if she was undressing in front of a man she didn't know and there was someone outside the door who might catch her. This time she counted the lightning strikes in her head. She and her daughter would always count out loud, and when the storm passed and the sky brightened, she was sad. The air thinned, the dogs poked their heads out of their kennels, the plants slowly picked themselves up, and Agnieszka felt as if someone had abandoned her. After the eighth strike, she heard the faint sound of a siren, smoke appeared on the horizon, the storm was gathering strength and a wall of rain obscured the view.

"It's from our direction," she said quietly and immediately started running.

Adam was shouting, but she couldn't hear him, didn't

even turn around. Rain flooded her eyes, she gasped for air, she felt as if she was under water. She stumbled a few times on the road, bits of gravel dug into the skin of her knees and hands, she felt no pain. Almost everyone was running after her, though she didn't know it. The blare of the sirens struggled to cut through the pounding of the rain, it sounded like a musical spinning top that hadn't been wound up tightly enough. People were running from the fields, woods, meadows and hills like children when their mothers called them in from the looming night. Agnieszka arrived at the scene and started rummaging through the embers, picking up bits of glowing charcoal. Why is Franek carrying a log? she thought as he emerged from the smouldering house.

Everyone came, even from the surrounding villages, the procession stretched for over half a mile. Some wept, others furtively wiped away tears on their sleeves, and the rest just walked, their eyes glassy. The prayers carried like an echo on a quiet and peaceful Sunday, when everyone lay belly up and full of soup. The three sisters walked single file, the youngest, Zofia, quickening her pace every now and then, because she wanted to see the freshly dug grave. Franek grabbed her by the hand and pulled her back. Pilot was staggering slightly, but Andrzej and Henia grabbed him by the arms and led him all the way to the cemetery. Piotrek was thinking about a girl he'd seen at the fair a few weeks earlier. Her dark hair had gleamed in the sun, and her deep blue eyes had looked up at the sky, then down at her red high-heeled sandals. Konieczny was walking with his family, serious, constantly chastening his pregnant wife, who was slowing them down. Alicja Owczarowa was carrying hollyhocks and roses cut from her garden, and she turned again and again to see if the small black dog was following her. At Finesse bar, the Christmas lights flickered fast, then slow.

"Let's sing to them," said Agnieszka to the crowd.

Acknowledgements
(from the Polish edition)

Thank you to my loved ones, Grzegorz and Magda, for their presence and support. I'd also like to thank Grzegorz for doing the first reading, for our conversations about the book and countless trips to the Low Beskids (I know: I keep saying that next time we'll go somewhere else).

Thank you to my wonderful editor, Magda Budzińska, for her vigilance, leniency and invaluable help.

To my publisher, Monika Sznajderman, thank you above all for your kindness. But also for guiding me along forest roads that are not on any map, and for showing me landscapes that I thought could only be imagined.

I'd like to thank Andrzej Stasiuk for the abundance of valuable information about saws and working in the forest, which resulted in one of my characters getting a beautiful orange chainsaw, rather than just an axe.

Urszula Honek (b. 1987) is the author of four poetry books and one short story collection. Her work has been featured in both print and online journals, newspapers, magazines and literary publications. She is the winner of the Grand Prix of the Rainer Maria Rilke Poetry Competition, the Kraków UNESCO City of Literature Award, the Adam Włodek Award and the Stanisław Barańczak Award, as part of the Poznań Literary Prize. For *White Nights*, she was nominated for the International Grand Continent 2022 Award, the Witold Gombrowicz Literary Award and Polityka's Passport Award. In 2023, she won both the Conrad Award and the Kościelski Award, which is given to the most promising Polish writer under the age of 40. She was born in Racławice, near Gorlice.

Kate Webster is a translator of Polish to English, based in London. She has translated many short stories and essays for publication in anthologies and online media and, in September 2018, took part in the Emerging Translator Mentorship Programme organised by the National Centre for Writing, where she was mentored by Antonia Lloyd-Jones. In 2022, she published her first book-length translation, *The Map* by Barbara Sadurska, which was shortlisted for the Oxford-Weidenfeld Prize 2023. *White Nights* is her second book-length translation.